Murder
in the Holy City

Ben Greer

Texas Review Press
Huntsville, TX

FIRST EDITION, 2006

Requests for permission to reproduce material from this work should be sent
to:

Permissions
Texas Review Press
English Department
Sam Houston State University
Huntsville, TX 77341-2146

Acknowledgment

With very special thanks to Jim Booth (http:/ www.jimbooth.com)

for his painting *The Storm*, which is used on the cover of this book.

Cover painting, *The Storm*, by Jim Booth

Cover design by Paul Ruffin

Library of Congress Cataloging-in-Publication Data

Greer, Ben.
  Murder in the Holy City / Ben Greer.-- 1st ed.
      p. cm.
  ISBN-13: 978-1-881515-92-0 (pbk. : alk. paper) 1. Police--South
Carolina--Charleston--Fiction. 2. Revenge--Fiction. I. Title.
  PS3557.R399M87 2006
  813'.54--dc22
                                      2006001564

This book is for Kecia,
who found me with love.

Murder

in the Holy City

Prologue

Edisto Island, South Carolina

Having worked a long day in a thousand acres of green corn, Archibald Sims went into the backyard to leave his muddy boots at the steps of the great house called Bonnie Bay. He noticed what appeared to be several pieces of clothing within the boxwood maze. He saw a hand with the palm towards the sky.

Racing forward, he found his mother lying at the entrance gate. She was dead, though she hardly looked it. Her red hair was still coifed, her makeup intact and her soft eyes open. Her clothes had been ripped from her body, her high heels thrown several yards away. Screaming for help, he cradled her body in his arms, upon her face a look of odd determination.

Archibald Hampton Sims had been born into one of the most ancient and distinguished families in South Carolina. He had been raised on a plantation forty miles outside of Charleston. He led an exotic and privileged life as a child, being taught at home by tutors. His university years were spent at The University of South Carolina and Christ Church, Oxford. At an early age, he had become exactly what his parents wished him to be—a Lowcountry Gentleman. He read Greek and Latin, spoke French, foxtrotted and waltzed, fished and hunted. But none of it had prepared him for this.

The autopsy revealed that Mary Sims had probably been assaulted and asphyxiated. Her body was hard with rigor mortis, particularly the jaws, which could not be opened without disfiguring the face. Forensic science was almost nonexistent in South Carolina in 1972.

There were over two thousand people at Mary Sims' funeral, and she was laid to rest in St. Stephens churchyard in downtown Charleston.

During the next few days, Sims met with city detectives and police. They had no suspects, no clues, nothing. Sims decided to take on the investigation himself. He went to the coroner's office and began to study the various murders that had occurred in Charleston County over the years. He read for seven to eight hours a day. He had never dreamed there was such horror going on all around him: decapitation, evisceration, bludgeonings, all manner of evil. After three weeks of reading, Sims was ready to abandon his investigation until he came across a case in which he saw clear similarities with his mother's. He studied the pictures of the corpse. It was a middle aged man. His clothes had been torn from his body, and most signifcantly, on his face and mouth and lips, there was that rigidness, that utter harshness, that he had seen upon his mother's face.

He left the coroner's office and drove back to Bonnie Bay. He walked around to the side of the house and entered the green boxwoods. Getting down on his hands and knees, he searched the ground, then spread the stiff boxwood branches, searching for any sign. About eighty feet away, he noticed the pine trees. They were over a hundred years old. He approached them. There were four. He studied the trunks and the bases of the trees. At the bottom of the last pine, he found what he was looking for.

He called the coroner and asked that his mother be disinterred.

The next day he stood in the City Morgue with a retired surgeon who worked for the police. Doctor Hobart was thin and small with a face as white as bone china. "You want me to what?"

"Examine her feet," Sims said.

"And then?"

"If I'm right, I'll ask for one more step."

"Are you sure your father agrees with this?"

"No, he doesn't, but he signed the papers."

Doctor Hobart shook his head and went into the examining room, followed by his assistant, a young man named Tom Tuttle.

Ten minutes later, Hobart returned, looking perplexed.

"Something's there, isn't it?" Sims asked.

"Yes."

"A burn?"

"We need to do another test to make sure, but it certainly looks like a burn."

"I read about a similar case. Try to open her mouth now."

"What?"

"I want to see if her jaws have been sealed together. And

if they have, then somehow you must get them open to look at her teeth, particularly her back molars."

"That will require an incision. Probably a big one."

"Then do it."

When Doctor Hobart came back, Sims sat in a chair, his face pale and his black eyes half lidded.

"The molars, the rear molars, have been welded together," Sims said.

"Exactly."

"Probably on both sides. Every tooth that had a silver filling and was near a similar tooth would bond in this catastrophe."

"What do you mean?"

"It was not murder, Doctor. It was lightning. A rogue bolt of lightning from a distant storm. It hit a pine tree first, then my mother. It ripped off her clothes, knocked off her shoes, and welded her teeth together."

Sims closed his eyes.

It was the beginning of a career.

1

Charleston, South Carolina

Thirty Years Later

Edward Finch was going to die tonight. It was not going to be pretty, but it was going to be original. This was what Goode had thought on other occasions, in other lands—if you can't be pretty at least be original.

Goode was standing in front of a fruit stand on Flood Street. A sign read: HONEY DEW MELON TWO DOLLAR EACH.

A black man dozed in a chair.

"Hello," Goode said quietly.

The man jumped and almost fell to the ground. He was wearing a yellow straw hat and galluses and a red shirt.

"Lordy, you startled me," the man said.

"I need a melon about this big." Goode used his hands.

"Oh, we got them lots bigger than that."

"No, this is good."

"Aw, come on, let me find you a decent melon, know what I'm saying?"

"Look, I need one the size of a man's head."

The black man looked at the mound of melons piled on a wooden table. He picked one out and handed it to Goode.

"That the right size?" the vendor asked.

"Yeah. Even looks like him."

"Like who?"

He smiled and paid him and got in his car. He drove across the Ashley River and took Highway 17 South towards the community called Hollywood. People here believed and practiced root medicine, voodoo. The neighborhood teemed with magic and spells and demons. Along the road were grim cement houses and rusting trailers and hovels rotting with mildew. Goode called this stretch of road Bloody Lane because it was littered with the bodies of dead dogs. He rolled up the windows in his car. The stench was terrible. Bloated bags of guts and bone rotting in the summer air.

There were vultures too. Great black birds that tore the dogs into pieces.

How ghastly, he thought. *How ghastly.*

He drove for another two miles and turned into a driveway. His home was narrow and wooden with the jambs of the windows and doors painted blue to keep the evil one out. *Or is it to keep the evil one in?* He grabbed the melon and stopped. It was still warm. He put the green melon against his face and smiled, then left the car and walked to his porch. He tapped the front door three times and opened it. When he shut the door, he made three little crosses on it.

The place was a dump. Junk furniture, peeling walls, rancid carpet. Once his home contained good Victorian furniture, Aubusson rugs, and sterling silver.

"But they took all that," he said to himself. "They took all the beauty from my life."

He walked into the dining room: a lone table on which sat a box of latex gloves.

And now for a little revenge.

Six pictures hung on one wall. He had found them in several annuals and blown them up. He touched the round face of Edward Finch.

"What did you say to me? What were your exact words? 'And now, Goode, I'm afraid I'm going to have to explode your little delusion.' Well, now, I'm afraid I'm going to have to explode you."

He went into his dark bedroom, where the air conditioner wheezed and chattered. He opened one of the green trunks and felt a little burst of joy. He grabbed the crossbow and threw the backpack over his shoulder. Holding the melon, he went to the backyard.

He set everything down beneath a live oak tree. He got out the rope and threw it over a high limb, then put the end of the rope through a swivel and bound it fast. He tied a heavy bolt onto the end of the rope, held the melon, and screwed the bolt into it. Warm juice trickled down his fingers. He gave the suspended melon a good swing.

He picked up the crossbow and the pack and stepped off forty-six feet. Carefully, he drew three small arrows out of the pack. Two were painted green. One was red. He cranked the bowstring back, slipped in a green arrow, and took aim. He pulled the trigger and the crossbow snapped.

A miss.

"Damn it!" he yelled. He couldn't believe he missed. He had practiced this a hundred times. He was about to use another green arrow, then thought: *No, you'll only get one shot. No, you must make this work.* He slipped the red arrow into the slot.

This time he relaxed, slowed his breathing.

The crossbow cracked again and the arrow hit the melon dead center.

"That's it," he said. "That's it."

He tucked the crossbow under his arm and sat down on his back steps. He watched the big, fat melon swinging in the breeze.

This was the best part, just watching it, just enjoying it all. He didn't know how long he could wait tonight, but he hoped it would be a couple of minutes.

He reached into his pack and pulled out the remote.

He stared at the melon with the red arrow in it a moment longer, and then punched a button.

It exploded into chunks of rind and green meat.

"Eight forty-five tonight, Finch. Eight forty-five sharp."

2

Inspector Sims rushed through the front door, holding the peach flan he had baked at headquarters. He worried that he had used too much cinnamon.

Henry was standing in the great entrance hall. "How is it, Mister Hamp?"

"Oh, alright, I guess. Maybe too much cinnamon," Sims said.

"Now you know how that girl loves her cinnamon. You can't put too much cinnamon on nothing."

Cooper raced down one side of the staircase. "You got it?"

"Yeah, but I need somebody to taste it."

They walked side by side down the long hall towards the kitchen. Sims poked his head into the dining room. The table was decorated with his family's china and silver. Sims wanted everything perfect because he and Abbagail were celebrating their first anniversary tonight—their first year of dating. Things had gone fairly well, even though she was much younger than he. It had become a theme in his life—dating young women. He wanted Abbagail to be the last one. He wanted their relationship to work out.

Sims pushed open the door to the bright kitchen. He glanced at the bullet hole in the wall beside the stove. This was a bit of a compulsion. The murderer had shot at him and missed by three or four inches. Sims had had a number of scares over the years, but this had been the worst. He knew that Abby and Cooper were still not over it. Obviously, neither was he.

Pink came out of the pantry into the kitchen. She and Henry had been married forever. They had looked after Sims since he was a boy. Pink was wearing a yellow dress. She was barefoot as usual.

"You have your pie?" Pink asked, putting her hands on her large hips.

"It's a flan," Sims said.

"It is a peach pie and I don't know why in the world you went all the way to the station when you have a good kitchen here."

"Convection oven."

"This oven right here has cooked a lot of pies just fine."

Sims set the flan on a worktable. "Well, let's taste it."

He found a knife and cut a sliver.

Pink produced two forks and Sims looked at her.

"On my diet," she said.

Cooper took the first bite.

"Whoa," the boy said. "This is awesome."

Sims was rolling the soft confection around in his mouth. "Not too much cinnamon?"

"You know, Dad, sometimes you're really anal."

Sims looked at his son, then glanced at his watch—5:15 p.m.

"Hey, I gotta pick up Abby. Want to go?"

"Sure."

"Pink, can you hide this in the refrigerator?"

"Yep."

Sims looped his arm around Cooper's neck and they headed out the kitchen door to the garage.

This had been hard at first, being physical with his son. Alice had done all the nurturing, but after that awful afternoon he knew he must learn. And he had worked on it, trying to discern when to offer a hug instead of a handshake, or even a kiss if he felt the boy needed it. Things were better.

They got in the old Bentley and pulled out into the light traffic of East Bay Street. The July evening was beautiful, mid-eighties, a wind blowing off Charleston Harbor, making the leaves of the palmettos bash and clatter. Sims turned onto South Battery Street and passed White Point Gardens, where the big magnolias were blooming.

Cooper pointed at the Gardens. "Our illustrious ancestor," he said.

3

"Our illustrious ancestor, indeed." Sims smiled.

"Have you read all his poems?"

"Most of them."

"Abby loves them."

"I didn't know Abby had read him."

"It's like she's read every book."

There was a bust of William Gilmore Simms in White Point Gardens. He had been a distant cousin and a well-known South Carolina poet. Sims glanced at his son. His hair was very blond and his eyes very blue and across his cheeks lay a spattering of summer freckles.

Sims turned up Meeting and headed for Chalmers Street. Abbagail worked for Pope, Pope, and Pope Attorneys at Law. She was a librarian and in charge of their stacks. Sims had met her during the Maybank murders two years earlier. He thought her the most beautiful, intelligent, and gentle woman he had ever known.

Abbagail was standing in front of the law offices in a pose that Sims had come to love: arms folded across her stomach, head down and slightly to the left, her lovely bottom lip poked out as if considering the solution to some difficult problem.

He pulled to the curb and she awoke, her long, blond hair moving in the breeze.

The boy opened the car door and Abby peered inside.

"Well, now there are two handsome fellas," she said.

"Care to have dinner with us tonight?" Sims asked.

"Well, I don't know if it's quite proper for a lady to have dinner with two gentlemen."

"How about one gentleman and a kid?" Cooper said.

"And which one is the kid?"

Cooper laughed.

Abbagail got into the car.

An hour later Sims and Abby sat on the side porch facing a garden whose brick walls were covered with jasmine. The air was filled with sweetness. On a small table before them sat a Hennell wine cooler holding a bottle of Cristal. They had finished half of it.

"Do you remember our first date?" Abbagail asked.

"Yes. You were quite drunk," said Sims.

"I was drunk?"

"It's alright. Heavens, it was our very first evening together. Everyone's afraid of the long pauses."

"How many drinks had I downed?"

"Wasn't it five?"

"Six as I remember."

"Oh, yes, six. Something about hovering over a cadaver with Tuttle all day."

"You were cute though," Abbagail said. "You were wearing your blue bow tie and your white linen suit."

"I still feel bad about it. Going on a date with the most beautiful woman in the world completely smashed."

"Well, not completely," she said.

He poured two glasses of champagne.

"Here's to our first year," Sims said.

Abbagail touched his glass with hers.

After a sip, Sims reached inside his coat pocket. "By the way, I have a little something."

"Now Hamp, I told you not to get anything."

"Well, it's not any thing, it's a number of things."

He handed her a narrow box wrapped in gold paper.

Abbagail fiddled with the silver bow, then pulled away the paper.

Sims loved her carefulness, the way she creased and folded the paper. He wondered if all librarians were so punctilious.

"Pearls," she said.

"Mikimoto."

"Oh," she whispered, pulling out the necklace and slowly letting it overflow her left palm.

He took the pearls and put them around her neck and gave her a kiss.

His left arm tingled a bit.

Maybe just a little arthritis, Sims thought. *Maybe nothing at all.*

4

Goode was thinking how sweet it was that Finch's front porch was painted white. It was a canvas, a canvas upon which Edward Finch's brains would be splattered like a Pollock painting.

He parked his car along Ashley Avenue. It was a one-way street that would get him out of town and across the river quickly. He put his pack over his shoulder and pulled his black baseball hat low over his eyes. He wore khaki shorts and a tee shirt and sneakers. At ninety pounds, with a good tan and a toned body, he could pass for a student in summer school, even though he was middle aged. He walked up Wentworth. The College of Charleston was steaming in the heat.

He stopped and stared and drank in the beauty of the place: palmettos and live oaks hovered above the ancient buildings of the campus. The smell of magnolia blooms sweetened the air and the sprinklers chattered and jingled in a cool haze.

Motionless in twilight, he stared a while longer, then shook himself out of it. He glanced at his watch: 7:52 p.m. He had to get himself in place well before Finch sat down with his evening newspapers.

He took a left on St. Philip. Finch's house sat two hundred feet down on the left. It was Victorian with a white front porch and several pots of luxurious ferns. Directly across from it stood a shotgun house which had been partially refurbished and made into a dorm. The first two floors were full of students, but the third was still being completed. It was empty.

But not for long, Goode thought. *Soon it's going to be full—full of death, full of horror, full of me. Just me, just little, disposable, forgettable me.*

He pulled his backpack higher on his shoulder and disappeared between two houses. Behind them lay an alley which led to the dorm. It was almost full dark now, but he moved quickly. At the back of the dorm, he climbed the fire escape. As he neared the second floor, he saw a student sitting in a chair on the landing. He was wearing a baseball hat and shorts and drinking beer and smoking. Goode could smell the pot.

"Hey, dude, want a beer?" the student asked.

Goode was prepared for something like this. It was why he chose his wardrobe carefully. It was why he waited for the smooth dark. It was also why he had brought his stiletto.

"Geeze, man, thanks, but I'm sorta like late," Goode said.

"Where you going?"

"Second floor."

"You living up there?"

Goode thought about continuing up the stairs, but decided to play it cool.

"Just visiting a friend, man."

"Oh, yeah, like who?"

This question bothered him. It was too much. Actually, it was impolite. He stuck his hand into his pocket for his stiletto.

"You probably wouldn't know him."

"Yeah I would. I know most of the fellas up there. It wouldn't be Tommy Smith, would it?"

"No, it's not Tommy Smith."

"Well, that's good. Somebody needs to stomp that jerk. What an asshole, know what I'm saying?"

Goode could hear it now. The boy was drunk. He was slurring his words.

"Yeah, Tommy's a jerk."

"I mean he really is, man, just 'cause he's president of KA, know what I'm saying?"

"I know what you're saying."

"Hey, come on and drink a beer."

"No, got to go."

"Okay, take one with you."

The boy started feeling around in his cooler.

Goode pulled the stiletto out of his pocket and flipped the blade open. *Okay, sweetheart. Maybe it's just your time.*

The student found a beer, tried to push himself out of his chair, then sprawled onto the metal landing.

"Whoa!" he bellowed.

"Woe indeed," Goode muttered. "And how very close you came to it." He looked at the student, then climbed the steps towards the third floor, towards the little room across the street from the white canvas.

5

Abbagail Taylor was sitting in a dressing room in Sims' house. They had decided not to live together, so she kept a few clothes here. She was looking at the pearls around her neck. They were exquisite. The necklace was the third piece of jewelry that he had given her. All were indicative of his sophisticated taste. She thought herself a lucky woman to have met such a man.

There was a tap at Abbagail's door and Cooper pushed it open.

"I still can't tie this tie," he said.

She turned to look at the boy. He was shining like gold: blond hair and blue eyes and roses in his cheeks. He was wearing a new tuxedo.

"Don't you want your father to help you?"

"Not really."

Though she wasn't much older than Cooper, she had gotten along with him from the beginning. She had thought that he might resent her, but she had not noticed that sentiment in him. He was a good boy, rebellious at times, brooding at times, occasionally withdrawn. But she knew that anyone would become introspective if their mother had been suddenly and capriciously taken. Alice Sims had been killed in a plane crash. An instant death, but one which still troubled both son and father.

She finished the black, silk bow and patted his arm.

"Think I'll have a little champagne tonight," Cooper said.

"Oh, really?"

"Dad said I could."

"I don't think he said any such thing."

"Well, he will if I ask him."

"Oh, he will?"

"Yep."

"Then, go ahead."

"Will you put in a word for me?"

"I don't think you should be drinking champagne."

"Why?"

"Because you're too young."

"I bet you were drinking champagne when you were fifteen."

"No, I wasn't."

"What were you doing?"

"Smoking dope."

"Hey, maybe we could work a deal."

"Cooper?"

"Yo."

"Dinner is at nine."

After he had left the room, Abbagail took off her robe and slipped into the gold lamé dress she had chosen for the evening. She finished her makeup and put on gold earrings. They were a birthday present from Tom Tuttle. She wondered if he was still jealous of her. Hamp said that he had never been jealous, but she knew that they had been friends a long time and grew even closer after Alice's death.

She put on a pair of gold pumps and glanced in the mirror once more.

Descending the teakwood staircase, she could hear Hamp whistling in the bedroom. She loved to hear him whistle because it meant that he was happy. Actually it meant more than that. Whistling indicated that he was not haunted by some investigation. Over the past year she had occasionally seen him too quiet, in his eyes a look of doom. She had first seen the despair after he had returned from a two-hour postmortem of a child. He had been silent nearly a week.

Abbagail wanted Sims to retire from the police force. He was too sensitive for it. She had met some of his cop buddies and they seemed unbothered by all the mayhem and horror of the world, but she saw the toll it took on Sims.

She stepped into the vast dining room. A chandelier hung over the long table. Spode china and Georgian silver gleamed upon linen. At the far end of the room, Pink was polishing a silver platter on the buffet. This was another thing that Abbagail wanted to change: servants. She believed it was simply wrong to have servants. She knew that Henry and Pink had practically raised him, but that did not affect her certainty that "having help" was wrong. Yes, he treated them as if they were his family. Yes, he had given them a house and land at Bonnie Bay, and yes, he had educated their children, but it was not right and she wanted to end it.

Abbagail smelled a wonderful aroma then: peaches and cinnamon.

She stepped towards the buffet and Pink turned.

"You not supposed to be here, Miss Abbagail. You'll ruin your surprise."

"I think I know what it is," Abbagail said.

"He calls it flam."

"But it's really just peach pie."

"That's what I'm saying."

Abbagail smiled.

One thing she did not want to change was his love of cooking.

6

Jasper Goode popped on his latex gloves and opened the door. The lights were burning in the interior hallway and most of the other rooms. There was the wonderful smell of new paint and fresh lumber. He went down the hall and entered a room. It was cluttered with paint cans and ripped-out pipes and broken plaster. He stepped carefully towards the debris and made his way to the small bathroom. The workmen had finished it: new tiles and new shower and sink. He turned off the light and sat down on the closed toilet and looked out the window at Finch's front porch. The ceiling light on the porch was burning. The lovely ferns trembled in the breeze. The porch swing swung.

He looked at his watch. He had time to consider things.

Once he had hated it that Finch was so punctual, was so much a creature of habit. The old man was always two minutes early to work. He spent exactly fifty-eight minutes five days a week in his office. He ate his lunch in the canteen in exactly twenty minutes. Exactly this, exactly that. Goode remembered he had even used the word itself in their final conversation.

There had been some indication of trouble, but simply small things. He had no idea what was coming.

Edward Finch was sitting behind his desk wearing a hand-made English suit. His silver hair was combed straight. His face was immaculately shaven. Only his nose looked bad. It was bulbous, swollen, the tip of it purple with broken capillaries. The nose of a boozer.

"What is this exactly?" Finch asked, holding up Goode's folder.

"What?"

"What exactly is this?"

Goode was so astonished he didn't know what to say.

"Well, it's my work."

"Well, let me explode that little delusion right now. This is nothing more than typing."

Remembering the words, Goode felt himself shake with fury.

He took the pack off his shoulder and set it on the floor. He pulled out the various parts of the crossbow and began to assemble it.

In just over a minute the weapon was completely ready.

He laid four arrows on the floor below the windowsill: two red ones and two green ones. He placed the remote beside the arrows. He picked up the crossbow and tucked it into his shoulder and sighted the porch swing.

"Perfect," he whispered.

He put the crossbow on his knees and checked his watch: 8:28.

Just seventeen minutes until I explode the little delusion called Edward Finch.

Goode sat silently and listened. He could hear everything: students below, a leaking pipe, an insect tapping against a windowpane, even the creak of the pin in his leg. Listening was his greatest talent. He had developed it while working in the mine. It had protected him more than anything else. It had saved him from snakes, from bats, from cave-ins and sudden sinkholes. Listening was the only good thing that had come out of the hell of his childhood.

In the darkness below, on the sidewalk, there was a movement.

He leaned forward.

A man ran up the steps to Finch's house. He walked across the porch and pushed the doorbell.

He checked his watch: 8:35. He couldn't believe it. This would destroy his whole plan. He couldn't believe this guy was here at this moment.

The front door opened and Finch stepped halfway through and offered his hand.

Goode was transfixed. He had not laid eyes on Finch in almost two months now. He had not changed—still tall, still erect, still with that detached and slightly aloof expression on his face. The two men disappeared into the house.

He slammed his fist on the windowsill and silently cursed and cursed and cursed. How could this happen? How could this man appear from nowhere?

He slumped back against the toilet and covered his face with his hands.

He tried to compose himself. He began taking deep breaths, tried to think of a simple Latin verb to conjugate.

Amo. Yeah, that's cool. Work on it.

He had taken three years of Latin in college and had been good at it. During stressful times it calmed him.

Slowly, using all his will, he tried to start the verb.

But he couldn't, he just couldn't do it. This was the destruction of three months, one week, and two days of planning.

Suddenly, he knew what he must do.

Attack. Go after him. Let nothing stop you.

7

Goode leaned over to gather his arrows, but he was shaking too much. It was not fear, but anger that made him shake. He rested his elbows on his knees, put his head in his hands. He remembered being angry like this a lot of times, even when he was a boy. In fact maybe that was when the real anger started.

His father had gotten injured on a construction site and sued and received a modest settlement. With that money he bought a local gold mine. There was just one problem—the mine had not produced any gold in over a hundred years. Oh, there were a couple of nuggets once a year, but hardly enough for the family to live. Goode's father had enslaved his two young sons to work the mine. Jasper had toiled in the darkness from the age of nine until sixteen. Until the day he squirmed through a tiny shaft to find his father having sex with his brother. He watched them for a while.

They seemed to be enjoying it—both of them. The scene filled him with disgust and rage and he slipped up behind his father and drove a pickaxe through his head. He strangled his brother and collapsed the clay ceiling over their bodies.

Remembering this victory over perversion calmed him enough to gather his arrows and fill his pack. He didn't take the crossbow apart. It was night. He knew he could conceal it. Besides, he needed to use it quickly now.

He slipped down the dark fire escape and made his way across the street to Finch's house. He stopped and stood and listened. He could hear crickets in the yard, the wind moving through a stand of pampas grass, the voices of the two men coming through an open window.

He looked down the side of the house. All the windows were open. *See, there's a reason for everything.*

It was very helpful that Finch hated air conditioning.

He took off his pack. He carefully felt his arrows and pulled out one with a tiny notch near the tip. "You're so smart," he said to himself. "You always think ahead, you always prepare, even to hunt in the dark." He slipped the red arrow, the notched arrow, into the shaft and cranked back the string of the crossbow.

He could not see the visitor. At the moment, the guest was just out of sight while Finch was making drinks in the kitchen. Goode put the crossbow to his shoulder and sighted Finch. He could fire right now. Zap him this instant, but everything told him to wait.

Finch carried the drinks into the den. He handed one to his guest, who sat behind a fern. Goode still had not gotten a clear view of him.

He lowered his weapon and listened to the conversation. Maybe they would say something to let him know when to fire. *Oh, please, please say something awful. Say something just terrible.*

" . . . but as I noted earlier, the more profound question is whether she can tolerate the affair, not whether you can," Finch said.

"I know, I know, but what if she talks about it?"

"Is she happy with you?"

"Well, as happy as an eighteen-year-old narcissistic, crack smoking beauty can be."

"She smokes crack?"

"I think she smokes everything."

"Let's sit on the porch. It is unusually cool tonight," Finch said.

This is it. I gotta move fast.

8

Goode picked up his pack and quickly stepped towards a stand of pampas grass in the front yard. He was wildly excited. There was something else too. The voice, the guest sounded familiar.

He hid himself in the tall grass. He was going to be able to use the beautiful white canvas after all.

Finch walked out on the porch, followed by—Goode couldn't believe it—James Owens. Another one of the men he detested. In fact, Owens had been almost as sadistic as Finch. What had he said on that black day? "This report is so bad, I don't understand how you were even considered. But I will assure you of one thing, you will not remain among us."

Oh, how fabulous is my luck. How truly fabulous. Two on one night.

He was standing in the tall grass and trying to think carefully. He could not make a mistake. He had wanted to kill Finch first. This had been his plan, his complete focus for months, but it was not the smart thing to do now. The smart thing was to hit Owens because he was young and quick. If Owens saw Finch die, then he might very well make it inside to the phone before Goode could kill him. But if Goode took out Owens, he was sure Finch would stumble and fumble long enough for the *coups de grâce*.

Owens it is.

He was sitting in a rocking chair and holding a drink in his right hand, his legs extended before him.

Goode held the remote in the palm of his left hand and supported the stock of the crossbow. He put the weapon into his shoulder and got Owens in his sights. There was one more moment of angry regret. He had wanted to watch Finch roll around on the floor with the arrow stuck in his head. He had relished the scene for so long, but there would be no time for that tonight.

He slowed down his breathing, put his finger on the trigger, and squeezed.

The string snapped and the arrow struck Owens in the right ear. He was knocked out of his chair.

Finch twitched, but then froze.

Goode pressed the remote and Owens' head exploded. The burglar alarm went off.

Gore covered the white porch. Finch had been hit with some of it. He was wiping his eyes, screaming, and trying to get out of the swing.

Goode slipped another arrow into the slot and fired.

It struck Finch in the throat.

He pressed the remote. Nothing happened. He pressed several times, then looked down and saw that he had put in a green arrow, not a red one.

Finch made it to his feet. He was stumbling towards the front door, clawing at the arrow in his neck.

Goode took the stiletto out of his pocket and grabbed his pack. He was not going to let the old man get away. He sprinted to the porch. The alarm system was shrieking. He caught Finch by the back of the head and turned him around.

"Hello, my dear."

In Finch's eyes there was a wild recognition.

Goode slit his throat and the old man crashed to the floor.

Suddenly, he had a thought. He reached down and made a quick cut, then turned to Owens and made another.

He glanced around, then jumped off the porch. He landed and heard a snap in his ankle. He tried to run, but couldn't, so he limped down the dark sidewalk as fast as he could, heading for an alley.

Ahead, he saw a police car racing towards him.

9

Tom Tuttle burst through the dining room doors. "Archibald, Finch has been shot."

Sims was sitting at the table with Abbagail and Cooper. "What?"

"Heard a radio call from a black-and-white. Somebody's shot Finch and killed someone else."

Sims jumped up from the table. He kissed Abbagail on the cheek.

"Hamp?" she asked.

"I owe him so much, Abby."

Sims and Tuttle ran out of the house and jumped into Tuttle's car. They sped north on East Bay Street.

". . . I don't know, arrows and bombs," Tuttle was saying.

"What do you mean?"

"Finch got hit with an arrow. The other guy's head's all over the floor."

"What?"

"Torn off somehow."

"How could that happen?"

"I don't know."

"How's Finch?"

"EMS is on the way."

Tuttle skidded to a stop on the corner of Wentworth and St. Philip.

There were three police cars and an ambulance at Edward Finch's house.

They ran up the steps and Sims lost his footing on the porch and sprawled. He looked at his hands. They were smeared in blood. The whole porch was dripping with brains and fragments of bone. Beside the front door was a headless corpse. Tuttle offered Sims a hand and they nodded at two cops and entered the house.

Finch was lying on the floor. Two EMS technicians were working on him.

Sims was astonished to see an arrow sticking out of Finch's neck, a small green arrow.

He knelt down beside him and took his hand.

"You're going to be alright now," Sims said.

Finch tried to say something, his face bloody and agonized.

Sims leaned forward to listen and Finch signaled for pen and paper and Sims grabbed it from one of the EMTs. Finch tried to write, but then collapsed.

"Out of the way now, get out," one of the technicians said.

The other one pulled out a pair of paddles.

Sims knew he was dead. He stepped into the dining room where Tuttle was standing.

"An arrow?" Tuttle asked.

"Who's the guy on the front porch?"

Tuttle shrugged. "No I.D. on him."

"That's not a regular arrow," Sims said. "What is it?"

"Something different. Maybe a spear gun?"

A cop came in. "We got him cornered."

"Who?" Sims asked.

"A suspect. He was carrying something weird, like a stock, a rifle stock. He slugged Logan and ran into a dorm."

On the way out, Sims stopped and touched the silver hair of Edward Finch. Then he saw something, even with all the blood. Finch's right ear was missing.

The two men moved carefully across the porch, then ran down the dark street towards the dormitory.

Six police cars with blinking lights sat outside the three-story house.

Police Chief Bill Straw came up to Sims. "We got all the exits blocked. There are a couple of kids up there."

"In the dorm?" Sims asked.

"Yeah."

"Hostages?"

"I don't think so. They're on the other side of the house. Used a bullhorn, told them to lock their doors. We're going in."

"Me too."

"Listen, Hamp, this isn't . . . "

"I'm going," Sims said.

10

An armored car pulled up and the SWAT team jumped out. They were dressed in black, wearing Kevlar vests and carrying M-16's.

Sims listened. Here were seven or eight vehicles and fifteen armed men and it was almost completely silent. Only the sounds of muted radios, muttered conversation, the bells of St. Michael's striking 9:30, and a sea breeze spreading the branches of a live oak near the dorm. He and Tuttle were kneeling behind a police car.

"I just don't understand how his head was blown off," Sims said.

"Had to be something like a grenade."

"But wouldn't that have done more extensive damage?"

"Won't really know until the postmortem."

The SWAT team was getting instructions from Chief Straw, who was pointing at the dorm.

Sims thought of his last luncheon with Edward Finch. At seventy-two, he still seemed full of vigor, his mind bright and sharp as ever. They were discussing organic tomatoes.

Straw waved Sims over to the armored car.

"You can't go. I don't know what this guy's packing, understand?"

"Sure."

"I know you were close to Finch . . . "

"No problem."

Sims made his way back to Tuttle.

"I want to be part of this, Tom."

Sims reached into his shoulder holster and pulled out a Glock. He chambered a round.

The SWAT team was ready.

Straw gave the *go* sign.

The team raced across the dark lawn and up the steps.

Sims was right behind them.

"Hamp!" Straw yelled. "Hamp!"

The lead cop kicked the door open and the others fanned

out into the entrance hall. There were several rooms on the left and right. A stairway led to the second floor. Three cops went to the left and three to the right.

Sims was standing beside a large bookcase. He was studying the door at the head of the stairs. Across the top of it lay a narrow glass vent, which was open. There was no light on the other side of the glass, but Sims thought he saw some kind of movement. There was an odd noise and the bookcase exploded into splinters and glass and Sims felt something sting his face.

Several of the cops cursed and hit the floor.

Sims ran forward to the base of the steps and hid behind a column.

"Where is he?" someone was yelling.

"Top of the stairs," Sims said.

"What's he got? Grenades? He's got to have grenades."

No, not grenades, Sims was thinking. *Something small. Something specialized.*

Everyone became silent as the cops crawled around to face the room at the top.

Sims could hear Straw's voice yelling over a radio.

"What the hell was that?"

"We don't know," a cop said.

"You don't know?"

"Explosive. Some kind of explosive."

Sims was tight against the column, holding the Glock close to his face. He was trying to figure it out—what kind of weapon it was.

A voice called out from the vent of the glass. "Hey, down there."

Silence.

"Hey."

The voice was high and squeaky, almost effeminate.

"H-e-l-l-o-o-o?"

"We're listening," a cop said.

"I want to . . . have a colloquy."

Silence.

"Perhaps too many syllables? I want to talk."

Silence again.

"Me want speak."

"We'll be happy to entertain a colloquy," Sims said.

"Oooohhh, intelligence from below. Sweet. Well, I have

a little surprise. His name is Danny Boyd. He is a very bright young man."

"How do we know you're telling the truth?" Sims asked. He was thinking that it was a trick, a way to gain time. Straw said the students were on the other side of the dorm.

"Um, this is Danny? Danny Boyd? I'm up here?"

11

A cop darted up beside him.

"We got to get a negotiator."

"Yes," Sims said.

"I mean, you're not trained, are you?"

"No, go get him."

The cop crawled back towards the door.

"He's going to get a negotiator," Sims called out.

"Oh, I'd rather talk with you."

"Frankly, I'm not trained."

"Frankly, neither am I. This is a difficult situation. I'll tell you what. There is something I want you to do. I've written a little note and stuck it in Danny's shirt pocket. I'll send him down."

"Fine."

"Does this seem like an odd thing to do?"

"Not really."

"Oh, come on. Of course it does. Giving up my hostage? Shouldn't I make you bargain for him?"

"Probably."

"Well, I baffle probability. I always have. So here comes Danny. And please, don't do anything rash. We don't want death from above, do we?"

The door opened and the boy stepped out. He was tall and thin, wearing blue jeans and a Grateful Dead tee shirt. He put his right hand on a banister and slowly began to descend. His eyes were wide with terror.

Halfway down, the boy stopped. He was shaking.

"Come on, son. Take it easy," Sims whispered.

"I . . . I can't."

"Sure you can. Just one step at a time. He's not going to hurt you."

The boy loosened his grip on the banister and took another two steps.

There was the noise again and the boy screamed and grabbed his back. He collapsed, fell a few steps.

Sims reached towards him.

"Stop right there," said Goode. "It's not a mortal wound, but the next one will be if you don't listen."

Sims was only four or five feet away, but he couldn't risk it.

The boy was writhing on the steps, blood pouring down his arm.

"What do you want?" Sims asked.

"I want you to sing."

"You want me to sing?"

"Yeah. I want you to sing my little note. When you see the words you'll know the melody."

"Alright, I'm going to Danny."

Sims stuffed his pistol in his coat pocket and slowly went up the steps.

"What kind of voice do you have?"

Sims felt the boy's pulse—slow, very slow. He pulled the piece of paper out of his shirt pocket.

"Hey."

"Yes?"

"Are you a baritone? A bass?"

"Baritone, I guess."

"Oh, shoot. Well, try a falsetto. It sounds much better if you sing it tenor."

Sims looked at the words. He had expected some kind of message—not this. He knew the melody as soon as he read the first line.

"I'm waiting," Goode said.

"We need to get him some help. He's passed out."

"Sing."

Sims was thinking: *Where's the negotiator? Where the hell is he?* He glanced downstairs. The SWAT Team was still.

He started haltingly, thinking how utterly mad it was.

"Raindrops on roses and whiskers on kittens. Bright copper kettles . . . look, he's bleeding to death."

"Sing or I'll kill him."

Sims started again. "And warm woolen mittens. Brown paper packages tied up with strings. These are a few of my favorite things." While he was singing, he decided. It was the only way.

"When the dog bites . . . ." Sims lurched up the stairs, kicked open the door. A stepladder crashed against the floor. He held the pistol with both hands.

The room was empty. No doors, no windows, no shooter.

12

Sims' heart was beating so hard he could feel it in his eyes. For a second, for only a moment, he thought: *An apparition? Something supernatural?* Then he saw it in the wall behind him.

The cops stormed into the room shouting, "Get down, get down, get down!"

Chief Straw raced up behind them, turned to Sims. "Got him?"

"No."

"What do you mean, no? There's no way out of here."

"How's Danny?"

"In the ambulance. Where's the shooter?"

Sims nodded at the fireplace in the wall.

"Ah, come on," Straw said. He stepped over to the fireplace and looked inside. "It's impossible."

Sims squatted next to him, looked at the soot, cinders on the hearth. "He had me sing to give him time. He went straight up, knocked all this soot down climbing."

"He'd have to be tiny. He'd have to be the size of a child."

"Danny would know."

"Yeah, he would."

Sims and Tuttle went over the dorm room. A lab team dusted the ladder and everything else for prints, then started looking for fiber. Sims interviewed a neighbor, then he and Tuttle went back to Edward Finch's house. Two lab technicians were swabbing for DNA. The bodies had not been removed.

Sims saw Logan standing on the lawn in front of the house. He had a black eye.

"I don't know, I'd say the guy was five-two, five-three, a hundred and ten pounds," Logan said.

"He had a weapon?"

"He had something, I don't know what it was. It looked like a rifle stock to me."

"A crossbow?"

"No, I mean, I thought of that too. What with the arrows and all, but . . . there wasn't a what-do-you-call-it, a, you know, a bow. There was just a stock."

Tuttle came over. "We found another arrow," he said. "Pieces. I think it hit Owens, exploded."

Sims looked through the screen door at Finch. He didn't want to go inside. There had been too many of them over the years—too many mangled bodies. Now one of his best friends? He stood and stared at the dim form on the floor.

Tuttle put a hand on his shoulder.

"You know, sometimes I think it will all get better," Sims said, "that things will . . . get better. But they don't. I mean, this is a complete horror."

"You don't have to go in there, Archibald. I'll take care of it."

"No, no. I do."

Sims went into the house and knelt down by Finch. He looked at the arrow in his neck, wanted to pull it out. He put a hand on his head and said a prayer. *Please let him go to the place he didn't believe in.*

He opened his eyes and turned the dead face into that of a stranger.

Seargeant Cay approached. "That kid died," he said.

"What?" Sims asked.

"The kid, the hostage. Died on the table at Roper."

Sims glanced at Tuttle, then looked into the blackness of the city.

"He could have told us more than anybody, I guess," Tuttle said.

"Yes."

"How old was he?"

"Oh, twenty, twenty-one. Listen, Tom, what do you make of the missing ear, of Finch's ear?"

"I don't know."

Sims looked at his watch—12:44 a.m. "I'm beat. Can you drop me by the house?"

13

It had taken Goode almost thirty minutes to scrub away the soot from his body. He taped up his ankle and shot up a little morphine.

At 1:15 a.m. he sat on his back porch listening to the tree frogs and thinking about his first brilliant success. To have gotten two of them at once was more than he could ever have hoped for. In a sense, it was luck, but he had also planned and prepared. Just as he was preparing for the others.

He remembered when he was a boy, growing up in the hill country of South Carolina. His father had taken him out of school, something which had shattered him. He really was a star in high school and his father had ruined it all by buying the mine and pushing him into it. Quickly, he had established a routine, laying out his tools: shovel, picks, goggles, gloves, a bright red lunch box into which he would put nuggets if he found any. Though he hated it with all his soul, he carefully prepared every morning to work the earth.

This obsession with precision had served him well in Vietnam. He had desperately wanted to join the Marines, but he was too small. Special Forces had accepted him. This made him proud, but he wanted more. He wanted to prove he was just as strong, just as tough as any guy in Nam. A buddy told him about the Rats.

They were sitting in his hooch and it was raining and he had just eaten a big bowl of rice and Nouc Mam sauce.

"I mean, man, if you want to be a hero, do it. You got the right size," Valance said.

"What's that mean?" Goode asked.

"You got to be little. That's why they call them rats."

"Tunnel rats."

"Yeah, it's really sort of far out. I mean, you get down in the gook's tunnels and go get him. It's just you and Charlie a hundred feet down in the dark."

"Wow."

"Yeah."

"You think they'd take me?"

"Take you? Hell, they'll probably give you a Silver Star for just signing up."

And sign up Goode did. Like most Special Forces, he was cross-trained: medic and sniper. The lifespan of a Tunnel Rat was about twelve weeks, but he had lasted eight months and made first lieutenant. Oh what lovely things he had done deep in the luscious dark. What splendid weapons he had learned to use. The very first was the crossbow. The Montagnards, the mountain people, had introduced him to it. He had zapped four or five gooks for sure, though one may have gotten away. It troubled him. It was inhumane, really. Even gooks deserved a certain death. He had to make sure it didn't happen again.

One rainy day he was lying in his hammock thinking about it. There was a loud blast somewhere beyond the perimeter of the firebase and it gave him the idea. He got an arrow and went down to see the weapons officer. He asked if there was any way to make it explode.

"Detcord," Sergeant Castles said.

"What's detcord?"

"Really groovy plastic, man. Just pack the shaft of the arrow, get you a cap, a little wire, and boom."

Goode was never uncertain about a crossbow kill again.

It was only one of the weapons he had used in the tunnels. There were others that were far more creative, far more original—like the thing that twisted in the dark.

His ankle twinged and brought him back to his porch. He could smell the rich pluff mud of the marsh and hear the wind moving through the cottonwoods. He was smiling. He was thinking about the twister. He had used it only three times in Nam and thought that he would never get the chance again. *Never say never. Never ever.* He had to have exactly the right kind of space: narrow, dark, confining.

He had already found it, of course. And he knew who would be in it and at what time. He also had found the place to buy the weapon. He had been there twice and spoken to the proprietor. He had even prepared his new set of tools: briefcase, stick, boots, and a ball of wire.

The next morning he got up early. He made some coffee, looked at the floaters in his small aquarium of alcohol. He went into the dining room. He studied the next victim's face and kissed it.

Oh, Ezra Whister, how you will love the twister.

14

Sims spent the entire day working the case. He went back to Finch's house for a couple of hours, then met with Ballistics and Prints at police headquarters. Around five o'clock in the afternoon he got a call from Tom Tuttle in the medical examiner's office.

"Williams says it's detcord," Tuttle said.

"Really."

"Found it in Owens' skull, pieces of the arrow."

"Call Professor Bates. Ask if there are any x-military guys on the faculty."

"One guy. Braggs. Out of the country."

"Examined Finch yet?" Sims asked.

"No. By the way, Owens's missing an ear too."

"The explosion?"

"No. Very neatly cut. Deliberately cut."

Sims was thinking about this as he left headquarters. He turned onto Bee Street, then zigged into Morris and slowly joined traffic on King Street. This was the commercial heart of Charleston. The buildings were shops, restaurants, galleries, and antique stores. All of them were filled with precious baubles or delectable foods or ancient furnishings. He rarely shopped here. The prices were absurd. He took a left and passed the great columns of the Slave Market. Hurricane Hugo had done much damage, but the renovation was almost complete and the grand building once again displayed the perfect lines of a Roman temple.

By the time Sims drove between the magnolias that stood beside the entrance to his home, it was 6:15.

He got out of the Bentley and stood in the thick heat of the July evening. There was not a breeze, not even a stir from the harbor, which was flat and hard and blue. The last of the magnolia blossoms were opening. He looked in the back of the car. The black ants were already pouring across the top of the seats, heading for the feeder beside the driveway.

As soon as Sims got in the front door, Cooper appeared.

"Dad, this thing is all over the news. Were you guys really close?"

"Yes."

"You used to hang with him, right?"

"Well, we had lunch once a month or so."

Cooper looked down, hung his head. "I'm sorry."

He tousled the boy's hair and moved towards the bar.

"Hey, Dad, I know this is not the best time, but I need to, you know, ask you something."

"Follow me."

The bar was a small room located next to the dining room. It had once been the office of Sims' father. It was paneled in rosewood. There were three or four big leather chairs and a long bar behind which hung a painting of Bonnie Bay.

Sims found a Waterford tumbler and poured himself a Glenmorangie neat.

"Want something?" Sims asked.

"I'll have what you're having."

He looked at his son.

"Hey, just messing with you. I'm never going to do that stuff."

"Oh?"

"Dude, my friends get so trashed. It's like—really embarrassing?"

"Please don't call me *dude*."

"Sorry. Um, look, there's something I really need to get."

"Okay."

"Pierced."

"What?"

"You know—pierced."

Sims looked at the silver ring in his son's eyebrow. He wondered how Alice would handle this.

"What else do you want pierced?"

"My tongue?"

"Your tongue?"

"It's really cool. Legare and Pitts got one."

"Let me understand this—you're going to get something stuck in your tongue?"

"Goes all the way through. Looks like a little silver ball."

"No, you're not going to do that."

"Why not?"

"Because it's—well, because, first of all it's ridiculous.

And secondly, it's got to be dangerous, unsanitary. It's your tongue, Cooper."

"That's right, it's my tongue—know what I'm saying? It's *my* tongue."

Cooper stormed out of the room nearly colliding with Pink.

He took a deeper swallow of whiskey. His throat burned to his belly.

"Did you hear what he wants pierced now?"

Pink was holding something. "You ought to let that boy pierce what he want to pierce."

Sims opened a can of salted pecans. "Why should I do that?"

"Seems to me you were doing a lot of nonsense yourself way back when."

"I was not sticking metal in my tongue."

"No, but you was sticking stuff on your tongue."

"Whose side are you on?"

"I ain't on nobody's side. I'm just telling you the way it was and the way it is."

He rolled his eyes to the right.

"And don't you be rolling your eyes at me. Miss Abbagail left this in the mailbox."

Pink handed him the card, turned up her big, round face, and eased from the room.

He opened the envelope, which had a scent: her perfume, Shalimar. The card was simple:

> Dear Hamp,
> I know this has been a terrible shock. I am so very
> sorry. I thought I would bring by dinner for you
> and Cooper tonight. Around 8:00? Call me if it isn't
> a good idea.
> Love,
> Abby

He smelled the card, then set it down on the bar. He finished his drink, thinking about her. She was the best woman he had met since Alice died. There had been three or four others, but each had some problem he couldn't endure: alcoholism, infidelity, irrational jealousy, even a sex change for heaven's sake. It had taken him a whole evening to discover that Vicki was in fact Victor, or at least had once been Victor. Now he always made sure a woman's Adam's apple was the size of a grape.

He went upstairs thinking how splendid it was to have a good woman in his life. She was a candle in the dark, a salve for the rawness of the universe.

15

Sims turned on the spigot in his enormous marble tub. It had been a birthday present to himself. He had always hated showers but was also tired of the usual small tub so he had ordered this beauty from Florence. Alice was mystified, Pink appalled, but Henry said, "If it don't work out, you can always use it for a duck pond."

He got in, sank down, and let the boiling water rise to the edge of his bottom lip. He lay completely still for a while, thinking about the day Finch told him he wanted to nominate him for a Rhodes Scholarship. It was the first time in his life anyone had told him that he was gifted. He remembered he was so startled that he thought Finch had confused his essays with those of someone else. He considered for a few moments, then got out.

He was not good at clothes. Alice had done all that for him. Over the years of their marriage she had bought him Armani suits and Alexander Julian shirts and Bally shoes—all the good stuff. Since her death he had slipped back into khaki pants and wash-and-wear shirts and loafers. Pink said he looked like a boat salesman.

He decided to do a little better tonight. He pulled on a pair of Lubiam trousers, a Burberry shirt, and a black pair of lace-ups by Allen-Edmonds.

He looked in his full-length mirror and smiled, but then felt sad. It was the way Alice used to make him look: beautiful.

Henry knocked on his door. "Miss Abbagail here with a box full of food."

Abby met him at the foot of the staircase. She put her hands behind her back, looking him up and down.

"Well, aren't we stylish tonight," she said.

"Think it's too much?" Sims asked.

"I think it's just perfect."

He kissed her and they held each other until she took his hand and guided him towards the kitchen.

"Hamp, do you mind if we eat in here tonight?"

"No, of course not."

It had always been his custom to eat in the dining room. He had done so since he was a boy, even breakfast. He loved china and old, knobby silver and Irish linen napkins that went from his belt buckle to below his knees. But he wanted Abby to be comfortable tonight and for many nights to come.

The kitchen table sat beside five floor-to-ceiling windows that had a view of the walled garden and the Charleston twilight. The table was made of cypress planks cut from trees at Bonnie Bay. There was a platter of boiled shrimp, coleslaw, and wedges of cantaloupe.

"I have one request," Abby said.

"Your request is my command."

"Can you make some of your hushpuppies? I think they would taste so good with everything."

"Absolutely."

Sims tied on a spattered apron and started to work. He filled a pot with Crisco, turned the burner on high, and quickly minced an onion.

"How can I help?" Abby asked.

"Try not to get in my line of vision."

"What?"

"If you get in my line of vision it takes my breath away and I can't concentrate."

She kissed his neck.

He made a batter of corn meal, eggs, milk, and sage, then tossed in the onions and mixed. He rolled balls and put them in the boiling grease.

He wiped his hands and turned. She looked so beautiful. She was wearing a white silk dress with spaghetti straps, her pearl necklace, and a pair of white leather heels. Her blond hair was lush, made almost white by the sun of the coast, which had also turned her skin to mocha.

"Hey, now," Abby said. "Don't stare. You'll make me blush."

He looked away, felt his heart race, felt almost like a kid.

Henry walked into the kitchen. He was wearing his usual dark blue suit, black tie, and white shirt.

"I'm sorry to bother you, Mister Hamp."

"Aw, we're just cooking some hushpuppies, Henry. What's up?"

"That ponytail man call me this evening. I forgot to tell you—that organic man? He said you certified."

"You're kidding."

"No, that's what he said."

"Certified for what?" Abby asked.

"Tomatoes down at Bonnie Bay. Didn't I tell you?"

"I remember something about tomatoes."

"I thought I told you about all that. I've been trying to get certified by the National Organic Association to grow organic tomatoes down on the island. I've been working on it for years. They have to do all these studies, everything short of drawing blood from me. But apparently they've certified the field. Right, Henry?"

"Yes, suh. Good night."

"Night, Henry." Sims clapped his hands and smiled. "This is just going to be splendid."

16

Abby sat down in a chair and lit a Marlboro Light. "I'm afraid I don't get it."

Sims glanced at the cigarette, then turned and began fishing the hushpuppies out of the oil. "I guess it's a couple of different things. For years I've felt like I haven't done my share for the environment. I mean, recycling and everything, but nothing substantial. And then there's all this land at Bonnie Bay that gets the usual crop rotation. So I thought, why not organic, grow something organic? Good for the earth. Good for people . . ."

"So you're going to grow organic tomatoes?"

"A hundred acres."

"Are you kidding?"

"Nope."

"And you're not going to use pesticide?"

He brought over the bowl of steaming hush puppies. "Heavens no."

"How will you keep the insects away?"

"Ladybugs," Sims said, throwing open his arms.

"Ladybugs?"

"Ladybugs eat everything: spiders, cutworms, aphids."

"And you think you can make a profit doing this?"

"Oh, that doesn't matter. What matters is growing organic produce. Imagine. We could just walk out into a great green field, pop off a tomato, and eat it. No washing. No worrying about poison. Nothing on it but rainwater and sunshine. Wouldn't that simply be splendid?"

Abby inhaled the Marlboro, closed her left eye against the smoke.

"And it's only the beginning. I want to plant corn, peppers, squash, eggplant. Do you know the topsoil on Edisto Island is fourteen inches deep? Fourteen inches. Why, I could change the world."

"Change the world?"

"Well, not change the world really, but I mean, I could change the island, change the way farmers think about growing food there. And who knows, maybe the idea would expand.

Farmers all across the nation might plant organic crops. Yeah, maybe I could change the world."

He saw a little smile on Abby's lips. He knew he had been gushing. It was a trait he didn't like in himself. If he really liked an idea, if he truly thought it was sound, he tended to gush, and gushing wasn't good. Or so his father had told him.

He set down the bowl of brown hush puppies beside the boiled shrimp and cantaloupe.

Abby was quiet and this bothered him a bit and she was still smoking, which bothered him a lot. He looked at the cigarette and asked her to pass the salt.

"Here you go," she said.

He raised his eyebrows.

"I'm going to finish this in just a second."

"I thought we agreed that you wouldn't smoke in the house."

"You agreed that I wouldn't smoke in the house."

"At least you could not smoke at table."

"At table?"

"Yes, at table."

"Is that some kind of British snip you learned at Oxford?"

"What do you mean?"

"At *the* table is what a normal person says."

"Fine. At least you could not smoke at *the* table."

She crushed the cigarette in an ashtray.

Sims felt his stomach shrivel. How had things gone so wrong, so suddenly?

They silently helped their plates. Abby got up and emptied her smoldering ashtray and returned.

"I'm sorry," she said. "I did agree not to smoke in the house."

"It's okay. I know it's a terrible addiction."

"Oh, so now I'm addicted?"

"No, no, I just meant . . . ."

She reached out and took his hand and kissed it. "I'm just kidding you, sweetheart. Listen, how are you doing with this Finch thing?"

He took a breath and looked at the shining blue of her eyes. "I'm not thinking about it. I'm forcing myself not to think about it."

"Good."

"I have this curious reaction to horrific events. At first, I don't feel them. It's almost as if they haven't happened. I'm clear headed, calm, able to function well. But then after a few days it all begins to settle in and I wake up at night and—do my little scream."

"And don't remember where you are."

"Yes, that's really odd—I wake up screaming and can't remember where I am. What do you think that's all about?"

"Conrad," she said.

"What?"

"Remember Kurtz in *Heart of Darkness*? 'The horror. The horror.' "

There was silence until the phone rang.

Sims answered. "Hello?"

"Gail there?"

"Who?"

"Gail."

"I'm afraid you have . . . "

"I guess you would call her Abbagail."

"Oh, just a moment."

He handed the phone to Abby.

"It's for you."

"Me?"

He nodded and noticed she seemed suddenly stricken.

"Hello," she said.

He tried to act interested in his food, but he could feel his heart beating. Her responses were quiet and only one or two words.

She hung up and looked at him with wide eyes.

"I have to go. I'm sorry. There's an emergency." She got up from the table.

"What is it? Can I help?"

"No, I'm terribly sorry." She grabbed her purse and ran down the hallway.

"Abby, what in the world is wrong?"

"I can't tell you. Not now. Not now."

He watched her dash out the front door.

17

Buzz. Buzz. Buzz. Buzz. Buzzing was on his mind.

Two days after his first sortie, Goode went into his garage and picked up his tools. He took off his shoes, pulled on the boots, set the briefcase and stick in the trunk. He pulled out onto Highway 162 and headed deeper into the steaming jungles of Hollywood.

Four miles down the road he saw the big sign: Crocodile City. Come and See. Three Dollars.

He pulled into the yard of the old Esso Station. Underneath a Chinaberry tree, Marshall Hicks was sitting in a chair fanning himself. He was immensely fat, wearing faded galluses, a dirty white shirt, and string tie. He was shoeless and flies swarmed around his yellow bare feet.

"Well, hello, captain," Hicks said. "Haven't seen you in a while."

"Getting the décor done, but I'm ready to start cooking now."

"What was the name of your restaurant?"

"Wild Things."

"Well, the price has gone up since I saw you. I'll need fifty bucks."

"I thought you said twenty-five."

"I got to thinking about it and he is a big ole fella. Fact, he's the biggest I ever seen."

Goode reached into his wallet and handed him the money.

"Just curious, captain. How you going to fix him, Italian dressing?"

"Bacon and onions and olive oil."

"Olive oil? Hell, you better use peanut oil. I never fried them myself, but that ole olive oil tastes too strong, seems to me."

"Peanut oil it is," Goode said.

"Hey, captain, you sure you know what you're doing?"

"I used to catch them when I was a kid."

The pit was located behind the gas station.

It was twenty feet deep and made of cement. Several pine trees stood in the center of it. They were dead. Goode sat down on a bench. He opened the briefcase, then closed it and opened it again to make sure it worked. He checked the loop at the end of the stick. Everything seemed to be okay. He had to be careful. He couldn't make a mistake.

He took a deep breath and started down the moldy ladder.

He was listening, waiting to hear the *buzz buzz buzz*, but he got all the way to the bottom and there was no sound at all. It surprised him, really, because he knew there were at least two dozen here. The pit was dark and damp. He looked around. There was a slimy pond in the center. Big rocks were scattered around. The air smelled rotten and heavy. He looked at his feet and shuffled forward. Then he heard it. Finally, he heard it. The *buzz*.

Carefully, he stepped back and looked above. It was lying in a mound of sinew on a ledge of boulder—an enormous diamondback rattler. His head was a huge triangle of fat and poison and fangs. It must have been four inches wide. The snake was staring at Goode and though he could not see it, he knew the black tongue was flicking in and out, discerning his intentions.

Keeping his eyes on him, Goode set down the briefcase, opened it with his left hand. He held the stick with both hands, putting his right finger on the trigger of the noose. He knew he had to be fast and he had to be accurate because if he didn't get him the first time it was all over. He bit his lip and held his breath and pulled the trigger.

Got him.

The mouth of the great rattler gaped open and he hissed and struggled. Goode pulled him from the boulder and the squirming weight almost knocked him off balance. On the ground the snake was trying to coil, trying to find a way to strike, his rattler buzzing shrilly. Using a dial below the trigger, Goode tightened the noose and the snake hissed even more violently. With a double-handed grip, he lifted it off the ground and shoved it headfirst into the briefcase. He held the head with the stick, then grabbed the dry body with his left hand and heaved all of it inside, relaxing the noose, snapping the briefcase shut.

The snake struck at the sides of leather and his rattlers were going.

Goode stood. Sweat was pouring down his face and he was

breathing hard. He let himself tremble. He let himself shake and listened to the rattler for two or three minutes.

Finally, the snake stopped striking and the buzzing ceased.

Still, Goode did not move, but began thinking. Ezra Whister's face floated into his mind and he began to smile, a real smile. "What a sweet surprise this will be for you," he whispered. "What a truly sweet surprise." He looked at his watch, pushed the illumination button: 7:50 p.m.

18

Goode climbed out of the pit, walked across the yard, and closed the gate behind him.

Hicks was still fanning himself. "Did you get him?"

"Yeah."

"When you cooking him?"

"Tonight."

"How about bringing me a piece?"

He nodded, opened the trunk of the car, and set the briefcase inside.

He got on 174 and headed towards Edisto Island.

Ezra Whister owned a house on the beach. It was built on sixteen-foot pilings secured by a cement slab. Near the back stairs stood an outside shower enclosed with cypress wood, a tall box with a door around which grew several oleander bushes. A perfect place for Goode.

It was 8:10 and the twilight was deepening. He parked the car in the lot at Conk's Restaurant. He sat and waited for the twilight to get to the edge of dark. He couldn't wait too long because he had to get into position before Whister came. He had been coming down every Friday and Saturday to stay at the beach house. He arrived, ran upstairs, then came down and took a quick swim in the sea. Afterwards, he bathed in the outside shower, opened the storage shed, pulled out the grill, and cranked it up.

He wouldn't be cranking up the grill tonight. He was going to have a swim and a shower, a long and cold shower.

At 8:20, Goode got out of the car and opened the trunk. He put on his gloves and got the stick and picked up the briefcase. The snake was still. He looked around to see if anyone had noticed him. A few people were entering the restaurant. Pelicans were flapping overhead and waves were breaking on the beach. Somewhere someone was playing the Stones' "I Can't Get No Satisfaction."

Yeah, I can, Goode thought and made his way to the oleanders beside the shower. Just as he sat the briefcase down, Whister's car pulled beneath the pilings of the house.

He got out, grabbed a suitcase from the trunk, and went up the stairs.

He unlatched the briefcase. This was the most dangerous point for him. Not for Ezra. The most dangerous point for him was coming up. Did he know it? Did he sense it in any way?

Goode got the stick ready and stepped about two feet away. He held the stick with both hands and pushed open the briefcase and waited.

Nothing.

He tapped the side. Still nothing. For a moment he wondered if it was still there. He even wondered if he had imagined all this. Was he going mad? Had he simply imagined that he had caught the snake and brought it here? He felt a chill creep across his skin, so he struck the briefcase.

The fat head slowly reared up. The snake was looking right at him. He could see its black eyes shining in the twilight. *Don't you look at me,* Goode thought. *Don't you try to hypnotize me.*

For a few seconds it just hovered there, the black tongue flicking out of its mouth and back over its head. Goode wanted to grab it now, but it needed to be farther out, more exposed.

A breeze rattled the oleanders and the snake turned and Goode swiped at it and missed. The snake lunged from the briefcase and knocked it over and raced across the sand towards the cement slab.

It had gotten away.

19

Goode couldn't believe he had missed him. *You stupid idiot, you stupid, stupid idiot.* He didn't know what to do. He was completely frozen and didn't know what to do. His heart was pounding so hard his throat hurt as he watched the snake slithering across the sand.

Overhead he heard Ezra Whister descending the stairs. He moved farther into the bushes and watched him run through the backyard towards the dark ocean.

All Goode's alarms were going off: *get out, get out, you blew it, it's all over, get out of here.* He steadied himself and saw the snake make the cement, where it suddenly stopped. Illuminated by the security light overhead, the rattler did not move. *Cool,* Goode thought. *The cement must be cool so he's just slowed way down.* Holding his stick, he moved out of the grass and crept towards him.

When he got ten feet away, the snake slowly moved. He stopped, watched it, and it stopped too.

Suddenly, Goode thought it was funny. The murderer was trying to catch his weapon. *I move and the snake moves. How funny, how completely funny. What do I do now? What do I say? Well, what about,* "Here kitty. Here kitty kitty kitty."

He started laughing, laughing so hard tears filled his eyes.

The snake glided across the cement and into the dark on the other side.

A car pulled up, maybe twenty feet from the direction the snake had disappeared.

Stunned at this surprise, Goode stood beneath the security light, holding his snake stick, laughing like hell, laughing like he was crying.

A huge, bald, fat guy got out of the car. He was wearing a Hawaiian shirt and a straw hat and was terribly sunburned.

"Sir," he asked. "Are you—alright?"

Goode wiped away his tears. "Oh, yes, yes, thank you. I just, um, lost my cat."

The man looked at his stick. "Your cat?"

"Yes."

"It's a terrible thing to lose a pet. Can I help?"

"No, no, I'll find him. Thank you though. Thank you very much."

The fat man glanced at the stick again and then walked towards the restaurant. As he disappeared into the dark, a dog he left in the car started barking.

The snake raced from beneath the car towards a corner of the cement. Goode got behind him and snagged his head in the noose. The rattlers exploded with noise.

He heard Ezra in the shower. He was singing and the water was thundering through the rusted pipes. Goode walked into the dark yard and stood beside the shower door. He found the latch and, using one hand, wrapped it with wire. The snake was rattling and hissing and so heavy he could barely control it.

He waited a moment, collected himself, then lifted the rattler over the shower wall and opened the noose.

The singing stopped. Goode ran to his car in the parking lot.

As he closed the door, he heard the screams.

20

Sims left early for his office in the old police headquarters on Line Street. It was paneled in antebellum oak and a window offered a view of Joe Riley Baseball Park. The other detectives worked in cubicles which surrounded an open area called the Fish Bowl. Here each detective's computer was networked and linked to its own big screen at the front of the room. When someone input new information, it immediately appeared on the central screens. He looked at them. They were nearly empty. He checked his e-mail. There was a report from the Crime Lab. Obviously lots of nuclear DNA had been found at Finch's house. It would take two weeks to process it.

He decided to call the case: Cupid. Not very imaginative, but it would work. He sat down at his desk and typed in the letters. Only two other screens held any information at all: a map of the city blinked two red lights where the homicides occurred. A second screen held around twenty digital photographs of the crime scene. These pictures could be enlarged and detailed by a detective at any computer.

It was grim stuff so early in the morning, but Sims punched up several photographs and zoomed them. He was studying the right side of Finch's head, thinking about the missing ear when Tuttle dashed into the room.

"We got another one," Tuttle said. His red hair was slick from a shower.

"Where?"

"Edisto Beach."

Sims reached for his gun.

They took Tuttle's car, blasted through morning traffic and hit Highway 174 heading towards the big, steamy island.

"Patrol car got a call twenty minutes ago," Tuttle said.

"From who?"

"A cook going into Conk's Restaurant. He said water was flooding the parking lot. He checked it out. Body in a shower."

"A shower?"

"Outside shower. House next door. Cook's hanging with the patrol officer."

"Any arrows?"

"No description yet."

Sims pulled out his cell phone. The M.E. was only a minute behind them.

By the time they pulled into the restaurant parking lot, a crowd was standing around the deputy's car. The cook led Sims and Tuttle to the body.

Ezra Whister lay white and wrinkled in a corner of the shower.

"Somebody tied him inside," the cook said. He was thin and smoking a cigarette.

"What do you mean?" Sims asked.

The cook pointed to the wire dangling from the latch of the door.

"See, they wrapped it from the outside. If you ask me, I'd say it's murder."

"Why would you say that?" Sims asked.

"Oh, come on. Dead guy locked in an outside shower?"

"Depends on how he died. Did you disturb the body in any way?"

"I just turned off the spigot."

"Did you know him?"

"He came in to eat once in a while. I knew his name. Whister."

"Stick around for a while."

"I got to cook breakfast."

"Please," Sims said.

The cook shrugged.

Sims stepped into the shower and squatted down beside the body. He saw no wounds or blood, but he did see that Whister's left arm was swollen and blue.

The M.E. came up behind him. "What we got?"

Sims backed out.

Pete Williams was wearing a white lab coat and carrying his bag.

"Have a look."

The medical examiner popped on a pair of latex gloves and stepped into the stall.

Sims and Tuttle watched while he went through a quick examination.

"Looks like his arm to me," Tuttle said. "Maybe he was shooting dope, OD'd."

"How about the latch?"

"Yeah, true."

"Look at this," Williams said.

The two detectives squeezed into the door.

Williams held up the left arm. It was about three times its regular size and blue. There was rigor mortis.

"Right here," Williams said. He pointed to the blue palm.

"I don't see anything," Sims said.

Using his left hand, Williams pulled a penlight out of his coat and illuminated the black punctures.

"Snake?" Sims asked.

"Looks like it."

"Whoa," Tuttle said.

"Odd that it would bite him on the hand," Sims said.

"He could have dropped a bar of soap. Or reached down to his calf. Anything. Snake hit him, then just slid away." Williams pointed at one of the drains cut in the bottom wall of the shower.

Sims was studying the concrete floor.

"Probably a moccasin," Williams said. "This island's alive with them."

"I don't think so," Sims said. He picked up something near the door.

Williams was flashing his penlight into Whister's eye.

Sims held the amber rectangle in his palm.

The medical examiner stood and turned. "What is that?"

"A rattle."

"A rattle? Oh."

"Rather large snake I'd say. Six feet, maybe more."

"Strange place for him to be. Rattlesnakes really avoid people places."

"Yes," Sims said. "They do."

21

At 9:00 that evening Goode entered the front doors of Roper Hospital. He was wearing a suit and tie. Around his neck was a toy stethoscope he had bought earlier in the day. It looked quite real. *Real enough for these fools anyway.*

He went past the quiet front desk to the elevator and took it to the basement. He had been to the morgue three years earlier when a buddy from Nam had been killed in a car wreck. Just before he got off the elevator, he opened his briefcase to make sure he had gloves and scalpels.

A guard was sitting at a desk in front of the stainless steel door.

Goode went straight to him. "Do you have an Ezra Whister?"

The guard was eating out of a Styrofoam bowl. He stopped, and picked up a clipboard. "Let me see. Whister . . . Whister . . . . Yep. Ezra Whister."

"I need to have a look at him."

"Sort of late, Doc."

"Just drove down from Greenville. Terrible accident. Sat on 26 for three hours," Goode said. He could smell the barbecue.

"I know how that goes. Got some I.D.?"

Goode reached into his pocket and pulled out the card.

The guard studied it and glanced up. "Never seen one like this."

"Just made it down at Kinko's."

The guard laughed. "Hey, don't be messing with me now."

"Yeah, the new ones don't look authentic at all. The old ones were quite distinguished. Budget cuts."

"Got a driver's license?"

Goode handed it over.

The guard compared the two pictures and handed back the cards. "Can I ask why you want to see the corpse?"

"He was the husband of a patient. I want to check out the cause of death myself."

"Oh, I can tell you that—snakebite. We haven't had one of those in years."

"Yeah, that's why I want to look. Rather hard to believe."

"Got people kind of shook up around here too."

"Oh?"

"Third professor to die in a week. The other two were murdered," the guard said. With the back of his hand, he wiped yellow barbecue sauce from his mouth.

"My practice is in Greenville. Haven't heard a thing about it."

"Please sign here," the guard said, handing over another clipboard.

Goode signed.

The guard led him to the door of the morgue.

"Hey, Doc. You got time to look at something on me?"

"Well," Goode said. "Yeah, sure."

The guard rolled up the sleeve of his shirt. He extended his hand.

"I had this thing about a month."

Goode looked at the lump in the man's wrist. "Does it hurt?"

"No, not really."

Goode turned the wrist from side to side. He palpated the mass of tissue. "Does that hurt?"

"Not at all."

"Ganglion cyst."

"Not a tumor or nothing?"

"No. Completely benign. Typically they grow along tendons. If it continues to grow, you can have it removed."

"Thanks, Doc. You know every time I see a lump, I'm thinking—the big *C.*" The guard punched numbers into a pad beside the door. "Listen, we're not going to have to stay in here long are we? The place gives me a headache almost every time, if it's more than ten minutes."

"We?"

"Yes, sir. Hospital rules."

"Oh."

"Security must be present unless there's an attending hospital physician or written permission from the M.E.'s office."

"Never heard of it."

"Sorry."

Goode looked at him. "I'm sorry, too."

The guard opened the door and Goode stepped into the

cold room. There was the smell of embalming fluid and Clorox on the floors and the other smell.

The guard led Goode to drawer eighteen and pulled it out. He checked the toe tag against his clipboard. "Yep. This is the rattlesnake man."

"Oh, how do you know it was a rattlesnake?"

"That's what Sims said."

Goode took his pack of scalpels out of his briefcase, set them beside the body. "Sims?"

"Detective Sims. He's running the case."

"Must be very intelligent."

"Yeah."

Goode tugged on his gloves and pulled back the sheet. For a moment, he stared at Ezra Whister.

"He was a son of a bitch, you know. A real son of a bitch," Goode said.

"Sir?"

"Oh, my daughter took a course from him at the College of Charleston. He was very difficult."

"Know what you mean. I almost failed out of there cause of a class called Deconstruction."

"Deconstruction?" Goode asked.

"Yeah, I'd never heard of it, but I guess you take something apart and then put it back together again."

Looking at the pale corpse with the blue arm, an idea sparked in Goode's mind. He took out a long-bladed scalpel, then palpated the shoulder joint. He made a quick cut below the clavicle.

The guard jumped, extended a hand over Whister's arm. "Hey, Doc, what are you doing?"

"Taking a trophy."

"Say what?"

"You see, I killed this man and I was in such a hurry I forgot to take a trophy."

The guard's eyes stared into Goode's. The scalpel struck even faster than a snake, into the right eye, deep, deep and hard, halfway up the shaft, right into the brain.

The man's mouth hung open for a moment, then he collapsed to the floor.

Goode removed the scalpel and stood and listened, listened hard, then he began working.

"Deconstruction," he murmured.

22

At 9:38 p.m. Sims was still in his office. He had spent the morning on Edisto Island interviewing the cook and others. The lab technicians had not lifted any clear prints from the scene. He wondered if Cupid was wearing gloves. Sims returned to Finch's and finally police headquarters. He was going over the day's events with Tuttle, who was playing with a letter opener.

"Why do you do that?" Sims felt his pager vibrate.

"Why do I do what?"

"You always have something in your hands. You're always playing with things."

Tuttle looked down at the jade opener. "I don't know. It's kind of a pet, a, I don't know the word, a—pettish."

"A what?"

"You know, something to pet, something to make you feel better—a pettish."

Though Tom Tuttle possessed a good mind, occasionally having trenchant insights into the human condition, his grasp of language was limited. He was famous for malapropisms.

"Fetish," Sims said.

"Well, I call it pettish."

"Well, you shouldn't say it because it makes you seem—inarticulate." Sims felt the pager again. He pulled it off his belt.

The message was simple: *Horror. Please help. County jail. Abby.*

Sims sprang from his chair.

"What's wrong?" Tuttle asked.

"Abby."

"Need me?"

"I'll call you."

Sims slapped his blue light on the dashboard and raced to the Charleston County Jail on Leeds Avenue. He jumped out of the car and saw an ambulance with lights flashing parked by the curb.

He got up the front steps and ran to the operation desk.

"Hello, Inspector," Buck White said.

"Abbagail Taylor called me?"

"Oh, yeah. Trouble down in Building C."

Sims ran towards Gate Two, which had already begun sliding open. He dashed by several cells, then saw the paramedics with a stretcher ahead. Abby was standing outside the cell. She looked so completely out of place here, so completely vulnerable. She was crying.

"Abby," Sims said. "What is it?"

She grabbed him, put her head against his chest.

"He's hanged himself."

"Who?"

"Jack. Jack."

Sims looked through the bars. He saw a shoelace dangling from a water pipe, a body on the floor. The EMS team was working on him.

Sims tried to walk her from the scene.

"No, I want to stay."

"Come on. These fellas know what they're doing."

He led her a few feet away. She wrapped her arms around him. "It's my fault. It's all my fault. I should have just bailed him out."

"Who?"

Abby held him a bit longer, then sighed and stood away.

"Jack Young," she said. "My son."

The EMS team was able to revive the boy. They put him on a stretcher. He tried to speak to his mother, but couldn't. Abby hugged him and the crew rolled him to the ambulance.

Twenty minutes later, Sims and Abby were sitting in the little bar at Eighty-two Queen.

"Jack called me at your house the night I ran out. He had been picked up—again."

"Oh, the guy asking for Gail?"

"That's what he's always called me. Even when he was a little boy. I always wanted him to call me Mom or Mama, but it was Gail."

Sims felt the shield slide in front of his heart. This is what happened when he sensed someone was about to hurt him, when a woman was about to hurt him. The bright, cold shield slid down allowing him to protect himself, allowing him to recede.

Abby reached out and touched his hands. "I'm very sorry. I should have told you about this from the beginning, but I was afraid. You know, single woman with child. I know how men look at it—baggage. So I didn't tell you. I just waited for the right time."

"Well, I think now's a pretty good time."

"Can I get another drink?"

"Bartender. Another round."

They were drinking martinis.

Abby pulled out a cigarette. Her hands were shaking so badly that Sims lit it for her. He remembered that once he had always lit a woman's cigarette.

Abby took a drag and blew the smoke away from him.

"I got pregnant when I was young. My parents wanted me to have an abortion, but good little Catholic girl that I was—I had the baby."

"What happened to the father?"

"Ricky Young? He stuck around for a while, then moved away. His father was in the Army."

"I think it took a lot of courage to have the baby."

"Probably just indoctrination."

The bartender put down the drinks.

Abby was staring into her martini.

Sims thought she looked beautiful. Her hair was a bit messed, her bottom lip seemed swollen from crying. She was wearing a black sheath dress with the pearls. Even in the darkness of the bar, her eyes seemed liquid and vulnerable.

"So why is Jack in jail?"

"Selling dope. I don't know. I tried to be a good mother. We lived with my parents so I could take part-time jobs. So I could be with him when he was a baby. He didn't give me a minute's trouble until he was ten or so. Then he started going haywire."

"It's when you begin to think—around then. If you are precocious."

"Oh, he's smart as a whip. He'll make a great criminal."

"I don't think that will happen."

"You don't?"

"There are a lot of programs—drug programs."

"Tell me about it. I've tried three or four already."

He wanted to say, "He needs a man in his life. He needs a man to hunt with, to fish with, to let him know his parameters." He wanted to say these things, but right now he couldn't. He had learned not to offer too much too soon once the person he loved had let him down.

"I should get back to the hospital," Abby said.

"I'll give you a ride."

"No. I'll take a cab."

"Abby."

"I know this hit you out of the blue. I know you don't like surprises. You need time to think. So do I."

23

By the time Sims got home, it was almost 11:00 p.m. Pink was sitting on the front porch, peeling shrimp.

"You're home mighty late," she said.

Sims sat down in a rocking chair beside her.

"Yeah, I'm late."

"How's the investigation?"

"No news really."

"Except that another professor got murdered today?"

"Ezra Whister, and I don't know if it was murder. Could have been an accident."

"Do you really believe that?"

"I don't know what to believe," he said.

"Something else is going on. I can hear that woman sound in your voice."

"What woman sound?"

"You know what I'm talking about. When things aren't going well in the woman department, you get this low down sound."

"Abby hit me with a surprise."

"What kind of surprise?"

"She's got a son."

"So do you."

"Hers just tried to hang himself."

"What?"

"He's a dope dealer. Got thrown in jail and tried to hang himself."

Pink was quiet. She rocked in her chair. The floor creaked. There was a west wind and the air was thick with the scent of pluff mud.

"What you going to make with the shrimp?" he asked.

"Jambalaya."

"Putting some andouille sausage in it?"

"I'm making my jambalaya, not yours."

"I think sausage adds something to it."

"It does—heartburn."

"Pink, I really thought I loved this girl."

"You do. Have you had your supper?"

"No."

"I thought so. Half this gloom and doom is proceeding from an empty belly. I made meatloaf and red rice and peas. Saved you a plate. I'm not talking anymore to you until you eat."

Sims found the plate of food in the refrigerator. He stuck it in the microwave for fifty seconds then sat down at the kitchen table. As soon as he took off the plastic wrap, he felt a blast of hunger. In two minutes, his plate was empty.

Suddenly he felt better. This was the way things had always been between him and Pink. She knew him. She understood him better than anyone in the world, certainly better than his mother.

He thought about her for a moment, something he rarely did. Sarah Manning Sims—first lady of the city of Charleston. President of the Saint Cecilia Society, President of the Gardening Club, President of the Daughters of the Confederacy and Daughters of the American Revolution. First in style, first in manners, but not first in the hearts of her family. She had been a cold wife and a cold mother who had said to him when he was ten years old, "You know, I never really wanted children. Your father did. He insisted actually, so if you must bond with someone, bond with him."

But he had not bonded with his father—it was Pink. She was the deepest and most gentle soul he had ever met in his life. She was also shrewd and principled. If he were wrong about something, her wit would cut him like a green switch.

Heading back for the porch, he sensed he might feel the sting of it tonight.

He sat down in a rocker beside her. The light from inside made shadows on the porch. "You need any help with the shrimp?" he asked.

"Just about done."

"By the way, where did you get them?"

"Mister Bell's."

"Always the best."

He was quiet. Maybe he did not need to talk about Abbagail. Maybe it was clear what he needed to do—end things now.

"So you're thinking about not seeing her anymore?"

Sometimes her abilities annoyed him. "I'm just thinking."

"This last year you seemed more like yourself to me. I mean, you never were Mister Sunshine, even when you were a boy. In fact, back then, I think you were worse."

"Worse about what?"

"Always thinking the worst was going to happen."

"I don't think I was that bad."

"Every pimple was a tumor, every cold tuberculosis."

"Well, I grew out of that."

"Excuse me?"

"Most of it."

"Abbagail reminds me of Alice in a way. She has that little knack of getting you out of yourself. Once you stop thinking about yourself, you're a pretty happy fella."

"I have been happy with her, happier."

"Then don't stop."

"Look, I feel betrayed. I feel that she should have told me about her son and all the trouble he's in."

"Probably should have, but she didn't. It's called making a mistake. Let it go. Quit analyzing it. Save that for the police work. Put these in the refrigerator. I am going to the house."

The house was her small brick bungalow, which sat behind the garage.

"Got your shoes on?" Sims called after her.

"No, and you ought to take yours off. Relax a little."

He sat in the rocking chair with the metal bowl of shrimp in his lap. He could smell their sweetness in the summer night.

24

Though exhausted, Sims lay wide awake at 4:30 a.m. He was thinking about Ezra Whister. There was one fact that made him want to exclude Whister from the Cupid case—no trophy had been taken. If an ear had been removed, then it was obviously murder and obviously the work of one man. Now the only connection was the fact that he was a professor.

The bedside phone rang.

"Hello?"

"Sorry to wake you up, Inspector . . . "

"I was awake anyway. Who is this?"

"Sergeant Blake. Look, I wouldn't call you but we got another homicide . . . "

"A professor?"

"Huh?"

"Is it a professor?"

"No, a security guard down at Roper."

Though he saw no immediate connection, he decided to go anyway.

Outside the entrance to the morgue was posted a rectangle of yellow police tape. Several uniformed officers stood around drinking coffee. One of them approached Sims.

"I'm Blake," he said.

He was overweight with a bright red face and bright black shoes.

Sims shook his hand. "Where's the body?"

Blake led him into the morgue.

The guard lay on the floor in a big pool of blood. On his face was a look of wonder. One eye was wide open, the other horribly mangled, as if something had gone in, had its look, and then come back out. He had never seen an eye look that way.

"An orderly found him about three o'clock this morning," Blake said.

Sims knelt down beside the body. He looked for anything resembling the other murders. A police photographer started taking pictures. A guy from the lab was measuring blood splatters.

"Did anyone see anything?" Sims asked.

"Just the orderly. He noticed the door was open and went inside and found him."

"What happened to his eye?"

Blake shrugged. "Something sure as hell did. But whatever went in didn't come out the back. I doubt it was a bullet."

"What's this man's name?"

Blake looked at a notebook. "Charles Baker. Worked here a long time."

"How long?"

"About twenty years."

"How do you know?"

"The orderly—Bob James—told me. He's still here, if you want to talk to him."

"Could you possibly get me a cup of coffee?" Sims asked.

"Sure enough." He turned to leave, then stopped. "Hey, do you mind if I ask you a question, Inspector?"

"Go ahead."

"Is that big ole mansion on the Battery, the Sims House, is that yours? I've heard that."

"Yes."

"Wow."

Sims nodded.

"I hear it's the biggest private house in Charleston."

"I think there're a couple of others bigger."

"How many square feet?"

"Too many."

"Guess you didn't buy that with police salary."

"No. I was lucky."

"Listen, I know this is asking a lot, but could I bring my mama to see it one day?"

"Sure. Saturdays are best. Give me a call."

"Cream and sugar?"

"Just cream. Mostly cream."

Sims watched the policeman leave. *I need to sell the place. It's not good for a cop to be living in a house like that. Well, not a house—home. It is my home.*

While he was thinking, his eyes were absorbing the morgue. He saw only one thing that seemed odd. One of the stainless steel drawers was not completely closed. He went over to it. Using his handkerchief, he pulled the drawer open, read the toe tag: Ezra W. Whister.

I wonder what the mathematical odds are of that

happening. One open drawer and it happens to hold Whister.

He pulled back the sheet and looked at the dead man's face. One of the eyes was open. It startled him. The pupil was dilated and turned to the left, as if looking at him, as if coolly, very coolly, sizing him up.

Sims reached and pushed down the eyelid. *Sleep now. Go back to sleep.*

He noticed something at the top of the shoulder, the rest of it beneath the sheet. It seemed to be a cut. He pulled the sheet away.

For just a second, he thought it was some kind of optical illusion. Bad lighting or some cold shadow.

But there was no doubt—the entire left arm had been cut away from the shoulder.

25

Dewees Island was to the north and east of Charleston. It had been bought by a wealthy investor who wanted to create a new kind of enclave: one which was completely green. No cars or trucks would be allowed on the island. There would be no stores or gas stations or movie theatres or anything else that reminded one of the developed world. There would be only houses, built from natural products and a maze of narrow paths upon which golf carts could take people from the landing to their solar- or wind-powered homes.

Goode loved it. He loved the whole place. Today was his fourth visit. He had caught the ferry from Charleston and brought along his briefcase. In it lay his tools: punji, scalpels, saw, needle and sutures, plastic wrap, and a waterproof rifle case.

He sat down on an outside seat in the beating sun. Usually he hated the sun, but today he was prepared for it: big straw hat, black glasses, and zinc cream, which covered his whole face. He had even tied a violet scarf about his neck. He was not going to be eaten by the sun.

Looking in one of the ferry's windows he caught a reflection of himself and laughed. *I look like Marlon Brando in* The Island of Doctor Moreau.

As the ferry cut through the currents, heading towards Dewees, he mused upon murder. He had decided to kill Professor Diane Howard-Smith now because she would be difficult to get to later. He liked the ferry, but it made things difficult. Right now he needed, he craved, simplicity.

On his first visit to the island, he had found her house in five minutes. She had been listed in the island phone directory and her name was on her mailbox. He had been able to observe her carefully that first day. She left for town at 9:00 and returned home around 2:00 p.m. It ticked him off really. All of them had fat, soft jobs, but hers was even fatter. Because she published meaningless articles in meaningless journals, her teaching load had been reduced to one course a semester. That meant she worked fifty minutes on Monday, Wednesday, and Friday. Throw in thirty minutes for office hours and she put in a grand total of 180 minutes a week at her job for which she was paid eighty grand a year—and, and, and—she got three months off in the summer!

It is outrageous, completely outrageous. I was supposed to have a job like that. Except I would have worked. I would have spent hours in my office with my students.

Goode pulled himself away from these thoughts. It didn't help him to go over this injustice. Besides, he had found an effective remedy: murder. Kill the ones who have hurt you and you will find joy and hopefully a little peace.

He got up and walked around the wheelhouse towards the bow of the ferry. There she was, sitting on a bench. Diane Howard-Smith. He couldn't believe it. He checked his watch— 12:10 p.m. She was going home early. He considered returning to the stern, but then thought, *No, she hasn't talked to me but twice in the last year, and she'll never know me in this lovely disguise. Let's have some fun.*

He sat down in a deck chair opposite her.

She looked like a bag lady. She was wearing a baseball cap, a white blouse, which was too small, revealing her hen-white belly. Below this were a denim skirt and a pair of sockless tennis shoes. Except for lipstick, she wore no makeup, and she was smoking a cigarette with her yellow right hand. Beside her sat a cloth bag stuffed with papers.

"I do love the ride over," Goode said.

Diane Howard-Smith sat.

"Especially on a day like today."

The professor's mouth was open, but she had not blinked once.

Her silence was beginning to annoy him. "I do wish they had more refreshments on this ferry, however. A cup of tea would be nice, wouldn't it?"

"I don't wish to engage in conversation."

"Oh, why not?"

"Because I am thinking."

"Is thinking hard for you?"

Diane Howard-Smith lifted her face and looked at him. "What did you say?"

"Is it hard for you to think?"

"Yes."

"Why?"

The professor took a drag off her cigarette and fixed him

with her small eyes. "Alright, you seem quite determined, so let's have a talk. What was your question?"

"Why is it hard for you to think?"

"Presently it is hard because I am thinking about the death of a very dear colleague."

"A professor?" Goode asked before he could stop himself.

"How did you know?"

"Well, I'm no detective, but your College of Charleston book bag . . . ."

"Oh, well. Yes."

"Was it sudden?"

"It was murder," she said.

"No."

"Haven't you read the papers?"

"I don't read them. They depress me."

Diane Howard-Smith took another drag and observed him. "Three members of my department have been killed. Two were murdered. The third was some kind of terrible accident."

The whistle of the ferry blew as it entered a small harbor.

She lit a new cigarette off the old one. "You don't live on Dewees, do you?"

"No, just visiting a friend."

The professor blinked and looked away.

When the ferry docked, Diane Howard-Smith strode to a golf cart and purred off towards her house.

Goode had a few hours to kill. Her walk didn't start until 4:00. He got in a golf cart and rolled away in the opposite direction.

He had come to love Dewees Island. Even in the lusciousness of summer it was a spare landscape. Hurricanes had stripped many of the trees. Here and there a pine would stand or even a live oak, but mostly the island was a series of tidal pools broken by the green of brambles.

After two hours of sightseeing, Goode secreted himself in a bank of blackberry bushes near Howard-Smith's house. He got things ready. He laid them out in the order he would need them: punji, scalpels, saw, needle and sutures, plastic wrap, gun case.

Once everything was set, he began picking blackberries. He was surprised to find that close to the ground the berries were enormous. He gathered a good handful and ate them. He conjugated a couple of Latin verbs, then went to sleep.

Goode woke with a start and looked at his watch: 3:50. He pried open a bush and there she was, right on time, heading his way. Or at least he thought it was the professor. She was walking barefoot down the sand road wearing something that looked like a burka: a white flowing headdress and long gown. She looked like a character from *Lawrence of Arabia*. She was carrying a straw basket.

Goode picked up his punji and assumed a squatting position.

26

She moved down the edge of the bushes. She was not smoking, and one hand held the basket while the other gathered berries.

Ten feet from Goode, she stopped, turned and looked back at the house.

Come on now. Whatever it is can wait. You need to get these berries before the birds do.

As if listening to him, as if hearing his thoughts, she started moving again, only a little faster. In two minutes, she was almost exactly over him. She leaned down, humming a song, her small eyes searching for the fruit.

Holding a bamboo needle between the thumb and index finger of each hand, Goode leapt from the bushes and drove the punji into her eyes.

Howard-Smith's mouth opened as if to scream, but then she fell.

Goode drug her into the brambles, laid her out near his gear. He took a moment to listen. There was only the sound of the island: a rising tide, the cry of gulls, cicadas. He extended her right arm from her body and got a scalpel.

He felt a rush of gratitude towards the security guard at Roper Hospital, but then this changed into self-loathing. *You should have thought of it. You are the Shelley scholar.*

Twenty minutes later, he was washed and clean and walking onto the ferry headed back for Charleston.

As it pulled away from the dock, one of the deck hands spoke to him.

"I didn't know they allowed hunting on Dewees."

Goode carried the full gun case under his arm. "Depends on what you're hunting for," he said.

"Really?"

"No, just taking my rifle to get it fixed."

"What kind is it?"

"Post-modern."

"Post what?"

He smiled. "Sorry. Most modern. It's a most modern piece—a .308."

The deckhand pulled a package of small screwdrivers from his back pocket. "I know guns. Bet I could save you a few bucks."

For just a second, Goode thought about unzipping the case and showing him. *Sweet old Tourette's. You shouldn't be thinking something like this. It's inappropriate.*

"Thank you, but my brother lives to work on these things. He was an ordnance officer in the Army."

The deckhand nodded and walked away.

When Goode got ashore, he jogged to his car, thinking the whole time. *Ice. You should have brought a cooler of ice in the trunk.*

"But it wouldn't fit in the cooler. Too long."

"You could have folded it, dummy."

"Oh, true, true, arms do fold."

Goode noticed a man sitting in a car next to him. The man was staring.

Goode raised a hand. "Oops. Arguing with myself in public. I must really work on that."

The man didn't smile.

Goode put his briefcase and the gun case in the trunk and drove away.

Fortunately, he knew where he was going. It wasn't far.

The Phat Fish store sat on Copper Street, just off Highway 17. Goode hated this part of town, with its grimy buildings and overgrown oleander bushes. He parked the car in the shade.

As soon as he walked into the store, there was the sound of trapped water: gurgles and gulps and bubbles. All around him were aquariums full of bright fish.

An attendant walked up to him. "Can I help you?" He was missing an arm.

Goode was a little shocked by it. He stared at the prosthetic, which ended in a double prong.

The attendant looked at him.

"Sorry," Goode said. "I, it's so hot, and I've been, in it, um, I need a tall aquarium."

"What kind of fish do you have?"

"Fish, yes, I have angel fish."

"Well, you don't need a vertical for them."

"I have a big house, tall ceilings and I really want a—vertical."

"Let me show you what we have."

Still rather bothered by the mechanical arm, he followed the man to the back of the store.

27

As soon as Sims had discovered the amputation, he made an appointment with Grover Atkins, president of the College of Charleston. The president was tall and solemn with white hair and brown eyes. They met at his residence on the edge of the campus.

"Now let me understand this, Detective Sims. You're saying that someone is targeting professors at this college?"

"Yes."

"Based on the murder of Finch and Owens."

"And Whister."

"But Whister was bitten by a snake."

"Deliberately put in his shower by the killer."

"How could you know that?"

"There is evidence that I have not released. The killer has taken a trophy from each of the men he killed, including Whister."

"What do you mean, a trophy?"

"A body part. He took an ear from each of the first two victims. This morning I discovered he cut an arm from Whister's body."

"What?"

"Apparently, he slipped into the morgue, killed the security guard, and cut off Whister's arm."

"Is there any chance you could be wrong? I mean, you're talking about a serial killer."

"Yes, there's a chance."

But Sims didn't believe it. He was quite sure what was happening.

Back at headquarters, the Fish Bowl was boiling.

Sims added five more detectives to the case. All the cubicles were filled. Phones were ringing, faxes chattering, beepers beeping.

Sims sat at his desk. He wore a blue Calvin Klein suit, polka dot tie by Bill Blass, Burberry white shirt, and Brooks Brothers lace-ups. He was deep in thought about the case.

Now that he was certain it was a serial killer, he had alerted every police agency in the state, as well as the F.B.I. He had never directed a serial killer investigation. He had been involved in two, but he had never been in charge. He was nervous. He wondered if he had the expertise to conduct this case. He worried if he could prevail. One of his assets was John Tyler. He had been an F.B.I. profiler for twenty years before he had retired in Charleston. Sims had known him socially, but never asked for his help. He had not needed it until now. Tyler was scheduled to come by at 10:00 a.m.

Tom Tuttle walked into the office. His red hair was badly combed. He threw down some pictures on the desk.

"Have you seen these?" Tuttle asked.

"No."

"Williams found something really weird."

Sims picked up the pictures. There were four color photographs of the armless shoulder of Edward Whister.

"You see what I'm talking about?"

"Yes."

"You do? I didn't. Williams had to show me."

Sims pointed them out. "He stitched up the artery and the veins."

"I can't believe you saw that."

"Professionally done as well. See this tie-off? The man has had surgical training."

"That's what Williams said. How did you know?"

Sims held up his hand. "Remember the cut? I was interested in the procedure. The surgeon was enlightening."

"I swear, I think you remember every word that was ever said to you."

"The question is why would he take the time to tie off veins and arteries in the shoulder of a dead man?" Sims turned in his chair and looked at the baseball park.

"Because he's crazy."

"And why would he use a snake to kill someone?"

"He did that to throw us off. I mean, he had been using arrows and detcord. He used the snake to bamboozle us."

"I don't think so," Sims said.

"Why not? In fact, it worked. He did bamboozle us—for a while."

"I don't think the snake was a decoy. It has another meaning."

"I guess you noticed Cupid didn't cut anything off of Charles Baker," Tuttle said.

"Right."

"Meaning Baker's death was just an accident. Wrong place at the wrong time. Baker probably caught him whacking off the arm, and our man used the same instrument to put his brain out like a light. Right through the eye—he knew exactly how to kill someone fast, even if he was caught by surprise."

Sims looked at Tuttle and smiled.

"I wish you wouldn't grin like that. Makes you look like William F. Buckley."

"I like William F. Buckley."

"You would."

John Tyler stood in the doorway. "Is this a brilliant colloquy between two forensic minds or can anyone join in?"

Tyler was short and round. He wore big glasses, blue jeans, and tennis shoes.

Sims rose to greet him.

"Have you heard the latest?" Tuttle asked.

He told Tyler about the sutures found in the corpse.

"Well, at least we know he's a psychopath now. That's helpful. I always get a little freaked when I think the killer's just mean and sane."

"Why's that?" Tuttle asked.

"If he's crazy he'll make mistakes. If he's not, he won't, or at least he'll make fewer."

"I hope you're right. Listen, I'm going down to the lab. See if the techies got anything new," Tuttle said.

"I'll come in a minute," Sims said.

Tyler pulled up a chair up. "So we got us a prof killer?"

"Indeed."

"Understand you were close to Finch?"

"He sent me to Oxford."

"What?"

"He nominated me for the Rhodes."

"You're a Rhodes Scholar?"

Sims looked at him.

"I didn't know that."

"All due to Finch."

John Tyler seemed a little bothered by this revelation. He scowled, blew out a breath. Sims had noticed it before. Intelligent men, ambitious men, were often agitated to learn that someone, anyone, had been a Rhodes Scholar.

28

"The sutures were professionally done. I think Cupid got his medical training in the military," Sims said.

"Why do you think that?"

Sims could feel a change in Tyler's demeanor, a distance.

"He used detcord in the first killings and he used a military expression."

"You talked to him?"

"When we had him penned up in the dorm."

"What did he say?"

"'Death from above.'"

"So you think we're dealing with a Vietnam vet?" Tyler asked.

"Some kind of vet."

The phone rang.

Sims picked it up.

"We got something really creepy," Tuttle said.

"What?"

"A blank fingerprint."

"I'm on my way."

Sims sat for a moment. It was something he had only read about, seen pictures of.

Tyler led the way to the lab. He seemed intent on doing it.

"You seem to know your way around," Sims said.

"Yeah, and I'm not a Rhodes Scholar."

Sims said nothing.

The lab was a bright, shining mess as usual. The white countertops were cluttered with Bunsen burners, microscopes, stacks of petri dishes, slides, bottles of stains and powders and acids.

Tuttle was standing in front of the fingerprint enlarger. The machine looked like a cross between an overhead projector and a microscope.

"The tech boys lifted this from the morgue drawer that Whister was in," Tuttle said.

Sims looked through the eyepiece. He could see edges of

swirl and a few lines, but the center of the print was a smear.

"Did they find any others?" Sims asked.

"Two others. Another index and a thumb."

Sims stepped away and Tyler had a look.

"Probably burned them all off," Tyler said.

"Would somebody do that?" Tuttle asked. "Would he put himself through all that pain? I mean, couldn't he just be really anal about wearing gloves?"

"Says a lot about him," Sims said. He went over to a coffee maker, found a glass beaker, and poured it halfway full.

"You're not going to drink that, are you?" Tyler asked.

"They make good coffee here."

"Yeah, but some residue could be in that beaker."

"Oh, he's done it for years," Tuttle said. "He's probably immune to everything in the lab."

Sims was sitting on a box of powder brushes sipping the coffee. His black eyes were large and bright and shining. "If he would be so careful as to burn away his fingerprints before he began the murders, then he is careful indeed."

"I really can't believe he did it," Tuttle said.

"How do you explain the blank prints?" Tyler asked.

"Well, they're not his."

"What?"

"A lot of people are in and out of the morgue, pulling the drawers. They could be somebody else's."

"Like who?" Tyler asked.

"Like somebody who burned their hands bad. Some kind of accident."

"Easily determined," Sims said. "We'll just fingerprint every-one who has had access to the morgue for the last two weeks. If everyone has normal prints, then we know these are Cupid's."

"Look, I'm going to the gym," Tuttle said.

"You're going to the gym?" Tyler asked.

"He thinks better on the treadmill," Sims said.

After he had left, Tyler sat down on a stool and pulled a notebook out of his back pocket. "I read the report you sent, made a few notes."

"Fire away," Sims said. The coffee did taste a little odd.

"Let's state the obvious. Cupid is little, five-one or five-two. A hundred pounds. White. Military. He hates professors, particularly College of Charleston professors. So he's not a serial killer in the classic sense. He's an agenda killer. Those guys did him wrong he's gotten even."

"Or, he's getting even."

John Tyler stood and adjusted his glasses. "My hunch is this is going to be a piece of cake."

"Why?"

"Agenda killers are almost always geographical. Typically they kill two to three people in a small area and then stop. Burn a little shoe leather and you should have this put together in two weeks flat."

Tyler gave a little salute and left.

Sims took a sip of the cold coffee. His arm tingled then. Sometimes it did this and nothing awful happened.

Sometimes.

29

Goode stepped into his dining room and felt a sudden burst of joy as he looked at the six photographs. He had actually done it. He had actually killed four of the monsters who had so wantonly ruined his life. It wasn't wishful thinking. It was action. Pure and precise and successful. He needed to get William Zeltner next. Goode didn't want to get him now. It broke the symmetry of things, but he had to do it. Professor number five would drive the cops crazy. They would start doing the big things then: roadblocks, news briefings, teams of investigators spreading into neighborhoods. All this would restrict his movements. But that was alright because after Zeltner, the remaining two would be in Charleston. One he had planned all along: Roger Neuman. He was the last of the portraits. The new victim, number seven, he needed to complete his desconstruction.

He turned on the television to catch the local noon news. The lead story was about a Charleston city councilman indicted for embezzlement.

They haven't found her. It's been two whole days and they haven't found her. What idiots. What complete bumbling idiots.

He went to his bedroom to sit in front of his mother's vanity. He clicked on the lights that lined the mirrors. Below them lay his assorted trick moles, moustaches, eyelashes, three wigs, lipstick, makeup, tattoos, and other things. He decided on a big mole with a red hair in the center of it and some false buckteeth.

There was one small problem. Zeltner had retired and moved to North Carolina and Goode did not know where in North Carolina. Not that it would be difficult to find out. He would just call the department, say he was a former student and wanted to write his dear old professor. They would immediately give him the address.

But I'm not going to call. I'm going to make a little visit to the English Department. It'll be more fun. And I need a little fun. I truly do.

He stuck the mole on his upper right cheekbone.

An hour later, he parked his car on Glebe Street. He got out, fed the meter, then stopped to stroke the smooth skin and admire the white blossoms of a crepe myrtle. The bark felt as silky and sinuous as the back of a young girl. He smiled. *Has anyone else thought of that?*

He walked down Glebe, crossed George Street, and entered the main square with the huge columns and russet bricks of Randolph Hall facing him.

How he loved this place. Everything about it—from magnolia trees and live oaks to the green grass and the wisteria vines whose muscular bodies looped around the pines. This was a place of quiet, a place of safety. How often in his three years of work here had he seen himself walking from his office to his class, his mind busy with the points he would make in his profound and moving lecture.

Once more he felt like weeping, weeping for all he had lost, for all they had taken from him.

That's right—you didn't lose it. You didn't do anything wrong. They took it. They raped you of it and then laughed, howled in laughter.

Goode took a right, crossed St. Philip Street, and passed Sottile Theatre. The English Department was located in Avalon Hall, right beside the theatre. He caught his reflection in the glass of the front door: his mole, his light coating of foundation, his beautiful rack of buckteeth.

At the main desk, he asked a secretary, who was slurping down a bowl of soup, if he could speak to Professor Zeltner.

She had a huge head and wore her hair in braids.

"He's gone," the secretary said.

"Oh?"

"He doesn't teach anymore. He retired."

"That's disappointing. He was my favorite professor. He helped my . . . my punctuation so much. Is there a way I could write him?"

Grudgingly she put down her noodle soup and opened up a file cabinet. She wrote down the address and handed it to him. William Zeltner, 42 Wire Lane, Hendersonville, North Carolina.

"Don't know the zip," she said. She turned back to her soup.

Just as Goode was preparing to go, two men were leaving an office. Chairman Chester Bates was trim as a leech and had a red face. As usual he spoke with only half his mouth. He was talking to a tall man who seemed familiar.

Goode broke his stare away from the men, acted as if he were reading the note. He was listening so hard he thought he felt his ears move forward.

"No one's been to her house, yet?" the tall man asked.

"Inspector, I think she's fine. Sometimes she just unplugs."

Inspector? Was this Inspector Archibald Sims?

"She unplugs?" Sims asked.

"Well, she's one of our finest scholars. Always has two or three articles going at once. Sometimes she just, as it were, *disengages*. I'll have someone check on her."

"Do you mind if I do it myself?"

"It's a bit of a trip. Dewees Island."

"I know Dewees. I used to take a johnboat out there when I was a boy. It has such beautiful tidal pools."

Chester Bates extended his hand. "Well, you'll call me then?"

Goode was studying Archibald Sims, examining everything he could: language, accent, tone, body movement, even scent. Bay Rum. He was wearing Bay Rum.

He wanted to say something, but managed not to.

30

Goode left Avalon Hall quickly and headed towards his car. He took a circuitous route and stopped occasionally to make sure Sims was not following him. The whole time he was thinking: *He's seen you now. Fine, he's seen you. You've seen him. The great Archibald Sims. The brilliant detective. We'll see who wins. We'll just see.*

Driving home, he tried not to think about it. He needed to go by a Barnes and Noble to get a city map of Hendersonville. The address hit him then: 42 Wire Lane. It would be a perfect way to kill Zeltner.

He got to his front door, tapped the lock three times with his right index finger, opened it, locked it back, and sealed it with the crosses.

He went to his bedroom, opened a trunk, and pulled out a silk bag. He loosened the drawstring and got the weapon. He laid it on the floor and stretched it out. How beautiful it was with its yellow handles made of elephant tusk. How truly beautiful. It made him think back to the last place he had used it—Pleiku.

It was a deep tunnel, but simple. There was a surface door fourteen inches wide, disguised as a tree stump. Then a vertical drop of six feet. The tunnel was long and straight, and the sides had been covered in water buffalo hide. Very unusual, but the man he was hunting was very unusual—Colonel Ho Ti Vet. One of the best snipers in Vietnam.

A spy had revealed the location of the tunnel and Goode had hidden himself in the small room at the end behind a silk screen covered with butterflies. Each one had been killed and then pinned upon the screen.

Goode had been expecting a collection. The profile on Vet said that he was a passionate lepidopterist. Still, when Goode's flashlight hit the butterflies and their beautiful wings, it startled him and even made him feel a bit sad, not for Vet, but for these lovely creatures of light.

He waited behind the screen for over nine hours before

Vet finally crept on all fours into the room. Goode heard him pause, listen, look, smell. Then he lit a lamp and set his rifle in a wooden stand.

Goode ran his finger across the wire of the garrote and took the handles in his hands.

Vet struck a match to light an alcohol stove on which he placed a brass teapot. He pulled off his backpack.

Goode was surprised. The profile said that Vet was thirty to thirty-five years old, but to him the sniper looked like a boy. Thick, black hair, clean-shaven, not one wrinkle or crease in his face.

Vet opened his pack and gently lifted a jar into the light.

Inside it, Goode saw some kind of motion, then color.

Vet held the jar up to the small lamp and smiled.

It was the most beautiful butterfly Goode had ever seen— shining wings, as if made of gold leaf, and a violet head.

Vet studied it a bit longer, then took a bottle holding clear liquid and an eyedropper from a shelf.

How can you do it? How can you kill these beautiful things?

Goode leapt from behind the screen and looped the garrote around his neck and twisted.

Somehow Vet managed to set the jar down. He struggled briefly.

Goode pulled the wire until he felt it saw into the neck vertebrae, then he relaxed. He sat for a while, looking at the butterfly in the jar. He poured himself a cup of hot tea.

When he finished the tea, he cut off Vet's right ear, stuck it in his pocket. He picked up the jar and made his way out.

In the jungle, a few feet from the tunnel, he opened the lid of the jar and let the golden butterfly flutter into the shadows.

He had not thought about the butterfly in a long time. It made him feel peaceful. He wondered if it was the only kind thing he had done in his life.

For a moment, for only a few seconds, he considered what he had become, then he began packing the other tools he would need.

31

Archibald Sims and Tom Tuttle took the 2:00 ferry to Dewees Island. They sat in the shade of the wheelhouse.

The heat was horrific, hammering down in waves from the white sun. Even the breeze of the sea did not lessen it.

Both men wore baseball hats and sunglasses.

"I think we ought to be able to wear Bermuda shorts in weather like this," Tuttle said.

Sims was thinking about Whister.

Tuttle held a letter opener. He was tapping his front teeth with it.

"You know you've got my letter opener," Sims said.

"Is this yours?"

"Yes."

"Mother used to call them my doodads. When I was a kid, some days I'd end up with a whole pocket full of things."

"It's a wonder you have a tooth left in your head."

The ferry pulled into the dock.

One of the groundskeepers was waiting. He directed them to a golf cart and drove to Diane Howard-Smith's home.

Like the other houses of the island, it was built on pilings. It had white siding and two picture windows facing the ocean.

The groundskeeper sat in the golf cart in the shade.

Sims tried the doorbell. When there was no answer, he knocked. He turned the doorknob, found it unlocked, and entered, calling out the professor's name.

A voice answered: "Yes?"

"Police Department," Sims said.

A woman appeared in a white dress. "Police Department?"

"I'm Inspector Sims. We're looking for Professor Howard-Smith."

"Sorry, I was vacuuming. She's not here," the woman said. She was smoking a small cigar.

"Have you seen her today?"

"No, but sometimes I don't see her. She leaves the door open for me to clean."

"She just leaves the door open?" Sims asked.

"Oh, the island's safe as it can be. Besides, she's not far."

Sims noticed three deep scars on her wrist as she raised the cigar to her lips.

"How do you mean that?" Tuttle asked.

"You cops. You always have this hard little edge to you. Couldn't you say, *pardon me*? Or *what did you say*?"

"Pardon me."

"Cute. Thank you for the courtesy. She likes the bay. She goes down there to medicate or something."

"Medicate?" Sims asked.

"Well, whatever it is. I think it's called medicate. Sits around crossed-legged with her palms open?"

"If she should return, would you please give her my card and ask her to call?"

The maid took the card. "Just follow the sand road in front of the house."

Sims and Tuttle walked down the middle of the road, feeling the scalding sand through their soles.

"Medicate," Tuttle said.

"What?"

"You'd think she would know the difference between medicate and meditate."

Sims was studying the sand. A recent rain had washed everything away.

As he turned a corner, he saw the first part of the bay. The water was shallow and still and blue. The skeletons of dead trees stood in the water beneath the beating sun.

The road turned again and Sims saw them—buzzards. A flock of them on the ground near some blackberry bushes.

"There," Sims said.

"Probably just a dead critter."

The men took off their jackets and broke into a jog.

Sims could smell it yards away—the peculiar sweet smell of a decomposing human being.

The buzzards shuffled and took off into the air, except for one. It was the largest, and it turned to stare.

"Get the hell on out of here," Tuttle said, waving his arms and running towards it.

The buzzard spread its wings and charged him.

Tuttle dodged behind a tree. "Did you see that?"

"It's feeding," said Sims.

"Well, it ain't feeding on me."

Sims could see the buzzard had something in its beak.

He reached down and grabbed a handful of hot sand and shells.

The bird rushed him and he threw the handful and the buzzard leapt into the breeze.

He stepped forward, squatted down to study what the bird had dropped.

It was a finger.

32

A thumb, to be more precise.

Looking into the blackberry bushes, Sims could make out something. He waded into them, covering his nose with his handkerchief. The body was bloated. Most of the clothes had been ripped away, and the skin had been burned by the sun. Her eyes shocked him. Sticking out of the sockets were two thin sticks.

He knelt down and peered into her face. The buzzards had ripped out the eyes, but he could see the wooden needles clearly.

Tuttle was comparing a photograph of Professor Howard-Smith to the corpse.

"That's her," Tuttle said.

"Seems so."

"God, what's sticking out of her eyes?"

"Punji."

"Say what?"

"Punji sticks. Some were small like these. Others large. The Viet Cong usually dug pits and placed them in the bottom."

"Maybe he used one on Baker."

Sims walked around to the other side of the corpse and bent over. "Tom, come over here."

Tuttle stepped beside him.

Sims lifted the right sleeve of the burka.

"Whoa, not again."

"He took the right arm this time."

Tuttle ran a hand through his hair.

Sims closed his eyes a moment.

Tuttle took his pen and prodded the sleeve. "Why is he doing this?"

Sims stared at the body.

"This guy's really looney tunes," Tuttle said.

"Get on the phone. I want every available officer to work this area. Everybody in the crime lab."

Sims took out his phone and dialed Chester Bates.

Two hours later, forty police officers and firemen had gathered in front of the professor's house. All of them wore plastic gloves and carried yellow evidence bags. Tuttle had given them their orders: move slowly, bag anything that even vaguely looked suspicious, drink a lot of water. They formed a line twenty-five men across and began moving through the yard and down the road.

Sims was standing beside the corpse and talking to Pete Williams. Both men wore blue masks and gloves.

"I'll have to get her to the lab, of course, but I'd say she's been dead at least thirty hours," Williams said.

"Yes."

"What I can't get over is these needles. You ever seen anything like them before?"

"I've read about them."

"You know what they remind me of? Pu-pu platter."

"Pardon?"

"You know, a pu-pu platter. Chinese food. They stick little pieces of cooked meat on them. Never touched it myself. Always heard it was cat."

Sims made the late afternoon ferry. During the ride across the sea, he was thinking about the instruments of death: cross-bow, snake, punji. All weapons used in Viet Nam.

The killer had served over there. Probably Special Forces because of his small size. He used unique weapons because he was a unique soldier. A man who went after the enemy underground, using the enemy's own weapons against him. A Tunnel Rat.

At the dock, a police car and driver took Sims to Chester Bates' office. Several other professors were waiting.

As soon as Sims walked into the room, he was hit with a barrage of questions. He held up his hands. "I can tell you very few things right now. In fact, I'm only prepared to say the following: The body is that of Professor Howard-Smith. The medical examiner says that she has been dead thirty hours or more."

"How did she die?" a bald man asked. He was wearing suspenders and a bow tie.

"Homicide. I cannot comment on anything else," Sims said.

"And why is that precisely?" the bald man asked, pressing the bridge of his wire rims.

"The investigation is ongoing. I do not want to reveal any fact that may jeopardize it."

"I am not one who enjoys this peregrination through police rhetoric. I insist on knowing the manner of my colleague's death," said a woman wearing a black suit and pink tam.

"Nor do I enjoy the badinage of intellectuals. I have investigated over seventy homicides. I am quite confident in my perspicacity," Sims said, with a bit of the superior air he remembered from his British education.

"But obviously," said the bald man, "we, that is, the English Department, are clearly targeted and clearly in danger."

"Yes," Sims said. "That is why tomorrow morning at nine o'clock, I would like to have a meeting with the whole Department to discuss matters of safety. Until then, everyone should be wary."

A few more questions were shouted, but Sims left the room quickly. He got in the police cruiser and asked the officer to drive him home.

He walked to his backyard in the summer twilight. The heat was fading because a breeze was blowing from the harbor. A wedge of brown pelicans flew over East Bay Street.

He felt as if each muscle of his body was stiff as a plank. He decided to start at the beginning. Opening Form would do very well to loosen him up. The posture required complete balance and more concentration than many of the others. He touched his tongue to the roof of his mouth and breathed through his nostrils and began to play Tai Chi.

33

Sims moved without stopping for almost thirty minutes. He thought of nothing, nothing but the form, the motion and perfecting it. When he finished, his mind was clean and smooth.

He sat down beside the Bentley and stared at the ants around the feeder.

He could hear Cooper approaching from behind.

"Hey, Dad?" his son asked softly. "Sorry to interrupt, but we were just about to eat some supper. You want some? Abby brought it over. I think she made it."

"Well of course, I made it," Abbagail said. She was standing on the back steps, wearing white cotton pants and a blue silk blouse.

Cooper ran up the steps and into the house.

"Should I have called first?" Abbagail asked.

"No."

"I'm so sorry about my . . . my complicated life."

Sims put his arms around her and pulled her close.

"Now, listen. I brought you supper because I know you need it. I'm going to go back home. You have too much to think about already."

"Please stay."

"Not tonight, darling. You need to be with Coop and Henry. Pink turned in early. Please eat and rest. Try not to think about all this horror."

"Did you hear about Professor Howard-Smith?"

"It's all over the news."

He sighed.

Abby brushed his hair back from his face. "Rest and eat and I'll call you tomorrow."

He went directly upstairs and took a cool shower. He scrubbed off the sun and sweat and some of the horror of the day.

He put on a pair of old Bermuda shorts and a worn Ralph Lauren shirt. He went downstairs barefoot, thinking that he was happy Abby did not stay. He wanted to be with her when things were not so tight. He knew she sensed that and he appreciated her for it.

Despite his informal dress, Sims was pleased to see dinner waiting beneath the Baccarat chandelier in the dining room. Elegance always soothed him.

There were two large Spode tureens. One held yellow rice and the other red beans and andouille sausage.

"This is awesome," Cooper said.

"You already tasted it?"

"Starving, dude."

"I am too," Sims said. He reached out for his son's hand and said a blessing. He knew this embarrassed Cooper, but he also knew it was good for both of them.

They ate quickly and took their plates to the kitchen, where Henry was washing up.

"How was the young lady's red beans?" Henry asked.

"Pretty good," Sims said.

"Coop says it was very good."

"Anything on a plate is good to Cooper."

"Hey, Dad, that's not true." He was sunburned and the freckles of his face seemed larger.

"Tell me one thing you don't like."

"Chicken bog. Yuk."

"Oh, that's right. You don't like chicken bog. Why is that?"

"All those bones and pieces of cartilage."

"Well maybe *you* should fix the chicken next time we eat it," Henry said.

"Gross. Hey, Dad, how about a game of eight ball?"

"You're on," Sims said.

"Mister Hamp, they got those tomato plants in the ground finally."

"I nearly forgot," Sims said. He was drying off the plates. Henry insisted the china should always be hand washed.

"You almost forgot about five thousand tomato plants? This case must be bad as everybody's saying."

Sims said nothing. He had trained himself to black out his work at home. Most of the time it worked.

By the time Sims got to the pool table, Cooper had the balls racked. Henry had gone home.

Sims flipped a coin. Cooper won and he ran the table.

"You've been practicing," Sims said.

"A little. Hey, when are we going striper fishing?"

"It's too hot. They're too deep."

"Oh, come on, Dad. You've been promising me this a long time."

Cooper was a competent outdoorsman at fifteen, but most of it was Lowcountry stuff: throwing a shrimp net, crabbing, flounder gigging. Sims had wanted to introduce his son to the fishing of the Upcountry. The best of this was striper and bass fishing. Although bluegill on a fly rod was an awful lot of fun.

"When the weather gets cooler," Sims said.

"You said we could go in the hottest part of the summer if we found some holes up in Lake Murray."

"That's true."

"How deep they gotta be?"

"Forty feet at least."

"Naw, really?"

"Maybe fifty."

Cooper racked the balls again. He broke them with a sharp crack.

"That's a nice stroke, Coop."

"It's this cue. I found it in the gun closet."

Sims smiled at the cream colored stick. "It was Mom's."

The boy stopped, looked at the stick as if it had moved in his hands.

In the silence, Sims thought he heard something in the front of the house. The floors were made of two-hundred-year-old oak. They popped and groaned with any movement.

"This was hers?" Cooper asked.

"Pure ivory. We got it on the trip to Kenya."

"That's not too cool."

"Here comes another politically correct lecture," Sims said. He had almost forgotten the sound, but heard it again.

"No, this is an animal rights lecture. Did you know elephants grieve their dead? They do. They . . . "

Sims put his finger to his lips, nodded towards the hallway.

"Oh, it's the boogieman," Cooper said.

Sims squinted his eyes, pressed his lips more emphatically.

This time there was a sustained creak on a certain board.

Someone was in the house.

34

Once before a madman had been here.

He looked at his son and could see the fear in his eyes. He motioned for him not to move.

Because of the previous invasion, Sims had hidden handguns around the house, on the back porch, even in the garage. A .38 lay in a drawer in the bookcase in the hall.

"Henry?" Sims called out.

Nothing. No response.

It's Cupid. I am hunting him. Now he is hunting me.

"Go to the kitchen," Sims whispered. "Call Tuttle."

"Dad, I don't want . . . "

"Go and stay put."

Cooper made his way through the series of doors that led to the kitchen.

While he was waiting for his son to escape, Sims heard someone quickly ascending the stairs.

Sims stepped across the room to the doorway.

Why would he go upstairs? Why would Cupid do that? Maybe it's someone else? But whoever it was would have heard my voice.

He looked into the hall, then to the stairs. He went to the bookcase and pulled out the .38. He checked to make sure it was loaded.

He put his fingers to his eyes. *Are you thinking right? Could it be someone besides Cupid? Don't make a mistake. This is the way innocents are killed. All the statistics agree. Abby? Could it be Abby? Some kind of joke? I have to try one more time.*

"Hey, Abby, that you?" he yelled out.

He turned his head and closed an eye in concentration.

Silence.

You could get Coop and leave. Wait outside for Tuttle.

"Not again," he whispered, "you'll not invade this house again."

Holding the .38 in the air beside his right ear, he went down the hall and started up the wide staircase.

At the top, he smelled something. Cigarettes. The smoke

smelled exactly like Abby's cigarettes. Her room, the room she used, was right at the top of the stairs. There was something else too—a sound, a tiny chatter.

What is going on? None of this makes any sense at all.

Lowering the pistol into position, but not cocking it, Sims inched into her doorway.

A boy sat in a chair. He was smoking and held his shoes in his left hand.

"Stepped in dog shit," he said. "Didn't want to ruin your rugs."

"Jack?" Sims asked.

"Whoa. What's with the piece, man?"

"What are you doing here?"

"Thought I'd drop in and see Gail."

"Didn't you hear me yelling?"

Jack pointed the shoes towards a headset around his neck.

Sims identified the source of the chatter. He kept the pistol on the barefoot boy, who wore blue jeans and a tee shirt that had printed on it BEEN THERE. DRANK THAT.

"Hey, I rang the doorbell. What else was I supposed to do? I ain't got your e-mail address."

It was true that the front doorbell didn't work. Still, this behavior was unacceptable.

"You should have announced yourself," Sims said.

"Oh, yeah? What should I have said?"

"That you were in my house."

Jack shrugged.

Sims saw that he had one blue eye and one brown one.

"Hey, where's Gail?"

"She's not here. She left some time ago." He stuck the pistol in his back pocket.

"Well, I'm glad to see you're not going to blow me away."

Sims said nothing.

"You know Gail told me about this little room. Said she keeps some things here. Is that true?"

"Yes."

"Mind if I try something on?"

"What?"

"Oh, a dress, a little dress would be really awesome."

"I meant, what are you talking about?"

"I know what *what* you meant."

They heard men pounding up the stairs.

"Archibald?" Tuttle yelled.

"I'm alright," Sims called back. "I'm in here."

Tuttle and a uniformed officer rushed into the room.

Jack took a drag off his cigarette and blew a smoke ring. "Wow. This your posse, man? This your posse?"

"Who is this?" Tuttle asked.

"This is Abby's son."

Suddenly Jack sprang out of the chair and lunged at Tuttle.

The detective never blinked.

"Hey, impressive," Jack said. "Nerves of steel and all that stuff."

"You're going to do that sort of thing once too often," Sims said.

Jack stood one foot from Tuttle with the butt of the cigarette smoldering in his mouth. "Oh, wouldn't that be a shame. An early and violent death."

"Sit back down in that chair," Tuttle said.

Jack wiggled his fingers in front of Tuttle's face. "Boogie-boogie-boogie. I'm really scared."

"Just do it," Tuttle said.

Still holding his New Balance shoes in his left hand, Jack snapped into a turn. With hands extended, he put one foot in front of the other as if walking a tightrope back to the chair.

Sims studied the boy, wondering how this incident would affect his sputtering relationship with Abbagail. He didn't want to let go of her. He really didn't.

35

"Formalin and lots of it," Goode said.

"How much is lots?"

"Eighty-one gallons exactly."

"Man, that *is* a lot."

"Yep."

"Mind if I ask what you need it for?"

"I'm cutting up people and preserving their pieces."

"Their pieces?"

"Body parts."

The clerk at Hipp Industrial Chemicals was short, fat, and slow. Finally, he laughed.

"That's perdy funny."

"I'm a perdy funny guy."

"You must be a taxidermist."

"Exactly."

Goode followed him down the aisle of the store. On either side of them stood black and gray and red barrels of chemicals. Most of them were marked with a skull and crossbones.

How wonderfully appropriate.

"What's the hardest thing you ever had to preserve?"

"Hippopotamus."

He stopped and turned to look at Goode.

"A hippopotamus? Really?"

"Yep."

"What'd you use on him?"

"Skill."

The clerk frowned, nodded, and moved on.

They stopped in front of two pallets holding several fifty-five-gallon drums.

"How much did you need?"

"Eighty-one gallons."

"Well, I'm gonna have to open one up and give you part of it."

"That's okay. I'll take them both. Never can tell, I may need some more."

"Thanks, Mister. I appreciate that."

"Oh, yes. I need a couple more things: two pounds of silver nitrate, alcohol, and an ultraviolet light."

Ten minutes later, he was riding up 26, headed for Hendersonville, North Carolina. He had decided to buy the formalin as soon as he crossed the state line, just to be careful. The drums sat in the trunk. The clerk had tied down the trunk door with wire. In the distance, the mountains looked like a long, blue wave. He rolled down the windows in the front of his car. The air was cool and without the fog of the Lowcountry. He took Exit 19 off the interstate and got on Highway 23. He was only five or six miles from 42 Wire Lane. He knew where the house was. Yes, he had studied the map, but mainly it was because of the GPS system he had in his head—a little something left from crawling around in the tunnels of Vietnam.

Goode's plan was to study the movements of William Zeltner for a day or so. It would be easy to do because Wire Lane was a country road running through Blotner State Forest. He could sit in the green safety of the woods and watch the professor's every move. Maybe he could even camp. That would be an unexpected joy. He could put up his little tent, get out the propane grill, and have some fun.

I could go to the store. Get hotdogs and burger and grill my dinner in the cool mountain woods.

But he didn't have a tent and he didn't have a grill. Oh well, this was not supposed to be fun. It was work.

The lovely, uncomplicated work of the damned.

He made a left turn, then a right and saw a sign reading BLOTNER STATE PARK.

He took another left and dead-ended into Wire Lane. He stopped. Great oak trees and sycamores grew on either side of the road.

Which way now? GPS says go left, young man, go left.

He made the left and drove several miles and saw a little stone house coming up. He stopped. Someone came out the front door and walked into the yard.

Can this be my beloved colleague?

He got out his binoculars. It was indeed. Still trim, still with his mane of auburn hair on which sat a golden yarmulke. He was wearing gloves and carrying a box of seedlings.

Goode watched him cross the yard, then kneel at a flower-bed beside the road. He actually had his back to the road.

Why I could take him right here. Right now. No prowling about in the woods. No sleeping in the car. I could snatch him up like a bird of prey this very minute.

36

"Now you need to calm down," Goode whispered to himself. "He's too big. Sure you could shoot him. Take out the old .308 and blow his big head off." But that was not the plan. The plan was the garrote and it simply wouldn't work here.

But it was so perfect, the whole scene: a lonely country lane, the professor in his yard, his back to the road.

He had to do it. No guts, no glory.

He took the garrote out of his briefcase in the front seat.

Now how to get him? I could just ease up in the car. No doubt Zeltner will hear the car approaching, turn, chat a little, and when he goes back to his work, I loop the garrote around his neck, twist and pop.

He put the car into drive and rolled down the road.

Twenty feet away, he was sure Zeltner was able to hear the car, but he didn't move.

Ten feet from him, there was still no acknowledgment of another presence.

Finally Goode stopped, put the car in park. He looked around.

What is this? Some kind of trick?

For some reason it made him mad. Zeltner was trying to trick him. Set him up in some way. *We will see.* He grabbed the garrote, left the car, and walked straight towards William Zeltner.

Goode stood behind him. The professor worked away, his hand spade cutting into the earth. Goode cleared his voice. Still nothing.

Is it some kind of mockery? Is he making fun of me? Or daring me?

He couldn't stand it anymore. He put the garrote behind his back and tapped him on the shoulder.

The professor flinched, turned, and stood up.

Goode saw them then. Hearing aids, one in each ear.

Zeltner reached up and turned them on.

"Hello," Goode said.

Zeltner was still fumbling with one of them.

"Yeah, sorry, these damnable machines." Zeltner turned his head to one side, adjusted a tiny knob, grimaced, then waved at Goode, signaling him to speak.

"Well, hello, I . . . ."

Zeltner smiled. "They're good, yes, very good. You can hear or not hear at will, but getting them to function is something different. May I help you?"

The professor's eyes were green, and he still wore his white goatee.

"I was looking for a place to camp," Goode said.

"There is a campground at the end of Wire Lane, the opposite direction you're traveling, but I wouldn't stay there."

"No?"

"Too many tourists. If I were you, I would find a spot in the woods. Use the campground showers, but find your own little place."

"Thanks. Good idea. By the way, what kind of flowers are you planting?"

"Portulacas. One of the few you can plant and see bloom in the summer. Excuse me, but I feel as though we've met."

"We have, actually."

"I was an English professor for thirty years. I just retired. You know, retiring is saying goodbye to the shore."

"I'm not sure I know what you mean."

Goode was figuring. *Six-two, six-three, two hundred pounds. Difficult, but not impossible.*

"Well, you're bidding adieu to all that you have known for your whole life: your work, your routine, in my case, even the town in which I lived for so long. I even miss the trees I walked by every day on campus. I'm sorry, nattering on. Now, you were on the staff?"

"I worked with you."

"Well, good heavens, you'd think I would remember that."

"Yes, you would."

37

The professor looked at him. "Wait, oh yes. I remember now . . . "

"Oh, you remember me now?"

"You? Heaven's no. What I remember is your terrible book."

Goode hurled himself upon him, slamming the handles of the garrote into his mouth. Blood went everywhere.

Zeltner fell backwards, stumbled to his knees.

He got behind him, looped the garrote around his neck and yanked.

Zeltner gagged, coughed and reached back with one hand.

Goode felt it grab him by the hair and throw him over the old man's shoulder to the ground.

Zeltner pulled the wire from his neck. He stood and wobbled towards the house.

Goode got up, grabbed the garrote. He was about to get it around his neck in the perfect position when Zeltner swung an arm out, striking him in his head with the butt of the spade.

He saw flashes of light, then hit the ground. He lay there a few seconds, trying to get up, but he couldn't. His knees were weak. Everything was blurry. He looked for Zeltner. The old man was opening the screen door.

He struggled to his feet, but by the time he made it to the door, Zeltner was inside, bolting it.

Get out. Get out now. You blew it. You completely blew it. RUN.

He raced to his car and jumped inside and started the engine. He burned rubber a hundred feet down the asphalt.

Two miles away, he was screaming. "Why did you do it? Why did you even try it? You crazy jerk. There was no chance. None. Now everything's lost. You'll never finish it, you'll never get the whole committee!"

The tears boiled out of his eyes. They were coming so hard that he couldn't drive. He pulled over and put his head on the steering wheel and cried so hard he thought he was going to vomit.

Then Goode heard something, a small voice: *Remember your Latin. Remember just one word. Remember* amo.

Alright, yes, amo. *The verb* to love.

He conjugated the verb through the past tense. At the end of it, his tears had stopped.

He was in control again and he knew he had to return. He was not going to let Zeltner ruin him. He simply was not.

He sped back down the road and parked his car behind Zeltner's house. Garrote in one hand, saw in the other, he ran to a large window that faced the backyard. He could see Zeltner throwing things, screaming: "Where's the phone, where is it?"

Get to him.

He tried two windows. Both were locked. He tried the back door. It was bolted, but there was a pet door in it. Very small. A door the size for a cat.

Or a rat.

Goode went to all fours, he knew things about tiny spaces. He blew out every ounce of air in himself, stuck his head through the door, then made his shoulders slowly dislocate.

In seconds, he entered the house, pulling his tools after him.

Zeltner was shouting into the phone, madly adjusting his hearing aids.

Goode crawled behind a sofa, got as close to him as he could.

When the professor hung up, he threw the garrote around his neck, twisted, planted his foot into Zeltner's back, and yanked with all his strength.

The old man's head popped off and clunked to the carpet, the body floundering to the floor.

He grabbed the bloody head by the ears and held it up.

"Now do you remember me? Do you? Do you? *Do you?*"

Goode kissed the head on the lips and set it on the kitchen counter.

He picked up his saw.

38

Sims was having breakfast with Abbagail at Hominy Grill on Rutledge Avenue.

"I couldn't do it," Sims said.

"Well, you should have," Abby said.

"Jack is obviously not well."

"Doesn't matter. This is a time for tough love if there ever was one."

"I don't know if I believe in that theory anyway."

"Hamp, he broke into your house . . . "

"The front door was open. The doorbell doesn't work."

"He was in your house, and you didn't know it. He was threatening. You should have pressed charges against him."

"The Bell Center will do him much more good. Sometimes things go wrong in a person's life. Sometimes you do things, even violent things, things that are not your true nature."

Abbagail reached out and took his hand in both of hers.

"I'm so sorry about it all," she said.

"It's alright." He glanced at her lovely face. She had been in the sun. In her tiny blouse, her skin was more brown, and her cheekbones bore the rouge of new sun.

"I really do think we can make a go of things," Abby said.

"So do I."

"Do you?"

"Yes."

"Even with my juvenile delinquent son?"

"I think I can help with him. It may sound sexist, but sometimes a male presence settles a kid down."

Abby kissed him.

After breakfast, Sims drove to the College of Charleston. He felt good about his decision to keep seeing Abby. He knew that Jack would complicate things, but there were always going to be complications in relationships. Everyone had baggage. Maybe his was not so obvious, but it was there. The years of being a cop, the dark rooms holding blood and corpses, had made him deeply pessimistic. If he were truly honest with himself, it was more than that—he had become afraid.

Now and again there was in him the brooding feeling that at any moment something terrible could happen to those he loved. There was only one act that could diminish this fear, one simple prayer: "God, help us. God, please help us." Whenever he said this, the fear abated. It did not go away entirely, but it did lessen.

At 8:30 he tapped on Professor Crow's door. The professor had asked to see Sims right after he had addressed the department, but things had been too busy.

Harvey Crow did not look or dress like the other professors. He was fat, wore his black hair down to his shoulders, and smoked a corncob pipe. On the walls of his cramped office hung two war bonnets and peace pipes, and there was a large picture of an Indian chief on the wall behind his desk.

"Native American literature," Sims said, extending his hand.

"Whoever thought you could make a living talking about wild Indians?" Crow said.

Sims pointed at the portrait. "Sitting Bull?"

"Crazy Horse."

"Ah."

"Have a seat."

Sims sat down in a willow chair covered with a black and red Navaho rug.

"How's the investigation going?"

"Slowly."

"This amputation thing really weirds me out. Any ideas about why he—if it *is* a he—is doing it?"

"A few, but right now I'd like to keep them to myself."

Crow pulled out a pouch of tobacco and filled his pipe. "I hope I'm not wasting your time, but when you said at the meeting the other day anything at all, I did think of something. It's not earthshaking, but it may be something."

Sims raised his eyebrows, opened his hands.

"Did you know that everyone who has been killed so far served on the same committee?"

"Committee?"

"Committees are the—what is the right word?—the, machinery of the Department. It's the method by which we get all the work of the Department done. There are five major committees. Finch, Owens, and the rest served on the Salary Committee. We serve on other committees as well."

"The Salary Committee?"

"Yes."

"And what does it do exactly?"

"At the end of each academic year, a professor hands in a report detailing his accomplishments. In part, whether or not he gets a raise is based on what the Salary Committee thinks of those accomplishments."

Crow struck a match and lit his pipe. "Could you close that door? I'm not supposed to do this, but Donald Smith next door smokes reefer twice a day, so . . . "

"A professor smokes marijuana in his office?"

"You're not going to bust him, are you?"

"No."

"Yeah, he takes a couple of tokes in the morning and afternoon. Hey, sometimes I join him."

"I see."

Crow puffed on his pipe. "Weird things go on in English Departments, Mister Sims. A lot weirder than doing a little pot."

"So, Finch, Owens, Whister, and Howard-Smith all served on this committee?"

"Yeah."

"Any other members?"

"William Zeltner was on it for years, but he retired spring semester."

"Would you say it's the most powerful committee in the department?"

"Let's put it this way: Some people make a hundred thousand a year and some make a third that."

Sims crossed his arms over his chest, squinted his left eye. "So a lot of faculty could have reservations about the members."

"Hate, I would call it. A lot of us hate them. Last year a fight broke out in a meeting."

"A fistfight?"

"Exactly."

"Between whom?"

"Edward Finch and Brian Braggs. He's retired military. Always using the military rap: *gung ho, squared away,* stuff like that. Irritates the hell out of most of us."

"I understand he's out of town," Sims said.

"Just got back."

39

Brian Braggs was in office 402 and opened the door before Sims could touch it.

"Inspector Sims, I saw you coming across the quad."

His handshake was too hard.

Sims assessed him quickly: a lean jock, maybe five-four, just over a hundred pounds.

Braggs stepped agilely backwards and extended his hand. "Please sit down."

The office was bare, neat, orderly. On one wall words were handprinted on a wooden slat: ENGLAND EXPECTS EVERY MAN TO DO HIS DUTY.

In a clear, plastic box, mounted and tilted at an angle sat a pair of worn Adidas.

Professor Braggs saw Sims glance at them.

"I was wearing them when I won the Boston Marathon."

"Impressive."

"I thought so. Beat out the chap from Nigeria."

"When was this?"

"Two years ago. No one else murdered, I hope."

"No."

"Too bad. There are a couple of people here who could use a little murdering."

Sims looked at him: flattop haircut, clean-shaven, a scar on his right cheek. He was a left hander. The killer was right.

"A rather provocative thing to say, Professor."

"Now see here, Inspector, there are a couple of things you need to know about me: I am direct, curt, and I do not suffer fools lightly."

"What do you teach?"

"Say again?"

"What is your field of study?"

"19th Century British Lit."

"I always loved Kipling."

"A silly twit who knew nothing of the military mind."

"I understand you retired from the military?"

"Incorrect. I served ten years as an Army captain and then resigned. The Army did not need me. That organization is quite exquisite. The best fighting force in the world. What needed me was this place. I joined the academic world to train young men to be *lugermench*. Are you familiar with the term?"

"Warrior poets?"

"Affirmative."

"I understand you slugged Edward Finch at a meeting?"

"I did."

"Why?"

"Because he refused to give me a raise for my new book."

"What was your new book?"

"A study of the British square in nineteenth-century novels."

"Why didn't Finch want to give you a raise?"

"The real reason is that he is, or was, a lily-livered, union-loving, effete communist. I bet you haven't heard that term in a while."

"Which one?"

"Communist. People think that communism ended with the fall of the Soviet Union, but they were quite wrong. The universities are packed with them. Utterly packed with them."

"You say that's the real reason. What was the reason he offered you?"

"That the publisher wasn't good enough."

"Who was the publisher?"

Brian Braggs stood up from his chair and threw his hands behind his back. "Look, let's cut the crap. You're here because you think I killed Finch, right?"

Driving back to the office, Sims was certain of three things: Brian Braggs had not killed Finch or any of the others, the Salary Committee was one of the keys to the case, and William Zeltner was next on the hit list.

Sitting at his desk, he called Zeltner at the number Charles Bates provided. No answer. No answering machine.

Tom Tuttle entered the office wearing a brown, linen suit that was two sizes too big. "The blank prints were the security guard's. Burned in a house fire."

"Is the plane available?"

"Probably."

"Book it for Hendersonville."

"Why Hendersonville?"

"We finally have a break."

Sims and Tuttle landed at the Asheville-Hendersonville Airport an hour and ten minutes later. To have driven the distance would have taken six hours.

Tuttle drove the rented car towards 42 Wire Lane while Sims navigated from a map.

They eased into William Zeltner's driveway. Sims put his Glock on the seat.

"Don't get that thing near me," Tuttle said.

"Of your many idiosyncrasies, the one that puzzles me most is your aversion to weapons. You are a nearly supernatural shot."

"Guns are evil. Now what do we say to this guy?"

"We go over the case thus far and then tell him to get out."

"What if he won't go?"

Sims picked up the package of photographs he had grabbed leaving the office. "Oh, I think he'll go."

The house was white clapboard with a large front porch. There were two chairs and a planter filled with ivy. A mailbox hung beside the screen door. Sims opened it and found a collection of bills. He rang the doorbell.

Tuttle put his back to the mailbox.

Sims opened the screen door and knocked.

"He could be on vacation," Tuttle said.

"Let's go around back."

Sims was observing. It all looked orderly. The grass had been mown. A side garden of tomatoes and squash was tended. As he approached the back of the house, his eyes were drawn to a pet entrance in the back door. It was smeared with blood. He pointed it out to Tuttle and went to the large window, pressing his face against the warm glass.

"Too late," Sims said.

"Huh?"

"Have a look."

Tuttle cupped a hand over his eyes and peered inside. "Oh my God."

40

Aware of local jurisdiction problems, Sims did not try to enter the house. He called the police.

Ten minutes later two officers arrived and kicked open the door: the black odor of death.

Within, Sims saw the worst scene in his career, in his life. On the kitchen countertop was a line of severed limbs: a leg, an arm, a leg, an arm, and, in a grotesque punctuation, a head.

The room was a marsh of blood and bits of tissue.

One of the policemen ran outside and vomited.

Sims looked around the room and then he understood. Cupid had taken another trophy.

He waited for the forensics team to arrive. He stayed a couple of hours to see if they picked up anything he had not found at the other crime sites. There was nothing—except the stitches. The sheer number of them. Cupid had tied off each arm and leg, even the neck.

Flying back to Charleston, Sims was completely silent while Tuttle rattled on.

"Cupid's gone crazy. I mean, he's gone completely nuts. Before, there was some kind of pattern. A couple ears, an arm, then another arm, but now—I mean, he's just hacking away. There's no rhyme or reason."

Sims was looking out the plane window.

"Well, what do you think? I mean, I agree that Cupid is Special Forces, but what about what we just saw?"

"I'm not sure."

"To do this kind of . . . of . . . well, carnage—one of your words—is, well, I'll say it again, looney tunes."

"I don't think so."

"You don't?"

"No."

"You don't think Cupid has just escalated this thing by about a hundred percent?"

"I think there is a pattern."

"You think there is a pattern?"

"Yes."

"What? What's the pattern?"

"Each time Cupid has taken something very specific, just as you pointed out."

"Yeah, but not this time."

"The torso."

"The what?"

"The trunk of the body."

Tuttle stuck his hands in his coat pockets, looked at the floor.

The plane hit a stretch of rough air.

"I don't believe it. I just don't believe somebody would go through all that butchery to—I mean, why didn't he take the head?"

"Doesn't fit the pattern."

"What pattern?"

"The one he is following."

"Which we don't see?"

"Not yet."

"I just don't agree with you. I really don't. I think Cupid has gone bananas, and it's just that simple."

"Well, there is one bright spot, possibly," Sims said.

"Yeah, right. What?"

"Maybe it's all over."

"Maybe what's all over?"

"The killing."

"Why would you think that?"

"Cupid got them all. The entire Salary Committee. Zeltner was the last one."

By the time Sims got home, it was almost 8:00. He walked up to his front door and touched the handle. He felt defeated. True, he had gotten a small break, but it was too late. He remembered his Tai Chi teacher then—Mister Zhang. *When your enemy is very strong, when his attack is ferocious, take his blows. Become soft. Absorb them all until he weakens. Then attack.*

He unlocked the door and stepped down the hall, taking a left into the study. He walked behind the bar and poured himself two inches of Glenmorangie. In a silver salver at the end of the bar was two days' worth of mail. He sat down on a stool and went through it, feeling the whiskey knocking away the tension in his back and neck. At the bottom of the pile was something from Abby.

He thought about not opening it, fearing that it might be bad news. Something told him it wasn't.

> Dear Hamp,
>
> Just wanted you to know that I've met with Jack's doctor. He seems like a kind man and very intelligent. He thinks Jack is severely depressed, but with medicine and therapy, can be helped. Maybe cured. Thank you so much. I would have put his little butt in jail.
>
> How are you, my darling? We need to get away soon. I would love to go down to Bonnie Bay. I think it would do us all good.
>
> Please think about it.
> Love,
> Abby

He put the letter beside his face. It was almost as if he could feel her gentleness.

41

Sims got up around 5:30 to see the early-morning news. The media had found out about Zeltner's murder. The first five minutes was report after report about the "Butcher of Avalon." He was happy that the mayor had decided to handle the press.

He showered, shaved, and put on an old khaki suit and weejuns.

At 6:30 a.m. the Fish Bowl was empty. He looked at the six computer screens. They were bright and busy with information, but there was no news from SBI in North Carolina. He had been hoping for some fiber or prints. He made some coffee and then went into his office and sat down, thinking about it all.

Are you finished, Cupid? Have you accomplished what you set out to do? Is your revenge finally complete?

He felt certain that Cupid was a faculty member. He had not had time to read all the interviews that had been done with professors. Perhaps the key was there. It had to be someone like Braggs. Someone not given a raise or not given praise or someone slighted and denigrated by the committee. He remembered that there were forty-two faculty members. He opened the computer folder. Forty-six interviews were listed. He decided to read a while and then call Chester Bates.

Sims got through seven interviews by 8:00 a.m. He was amazed by them. He had never had a case in which so many people so disliked their colleagues. He had never read so much envy, anger, spite, and complete rage in his life. In the English Department it seemed everyone hated everyone else. Still, he had not found a clue that might suggest someone was willing to murder a fellow colleague, let alone five.

He picked up the phone and called Bates, who answered immediately.

"I wanted first of all to offer my condolences . . . ," Sims began.

"Well, that's fine, that's fine, but what is going on? I mean, faculty are calling me day and night, and now this. What are you . . . "

Sims let him go on a while and then decided he needed a face-to-face.

When he walked into the chairman's office, Bates was sitting at his desk, his face red, his eyes swollen and twitching.

"This is madness. Absolute madness. Are these news reports correct? Did he dismember him?"

"Yes."

Bates put his hands to his face. "You've got to stop this, Sims. You've got to stop this. He's going to kill us all, every single one of us. Don't you see what's happening?"

Sims held up his hand. "Professor, professor, I want you to calm down . . . "

"I can't calm down. I haven't had any sleep in days. I have two colleagues in hospital and one at home having anxiety attacks. Why can't you stop these terrible events?"

"They have stopped."

"What?"

"I believe they have stopped."

Chester Bates collapsed in a chair. He put his left hand over an eye and shivered. "Why do you think that?"

Sims pulled a chair beside him and went over his thesis concerning the Salary Committee. He spoke quietly, evenly. At the end, Bates was calmer.

"So you think it's over," Bates said.

"Yes."

"But you are not certain?"

"I want everyone to stay vigilant. I'm keeping everything just as it is."

"What do you mean?"

"Plainclothesmen on campus, patrols . . . "

"What should I tell the faculty?"

"Don't tell them about the Salary Committee. Keep that completely to yourself. Say only that there is a break in the investigation."

The professor stood straight up. "I am not an incompetent. I am not. Do you understand?"

"Agenda murders are very difficult to break. Once you have the key, they seem simple, but that is always in retrospection."

Chester Bates seemed back in control. "So, do you have any suspects?"

"No."

"None?"

"No."

"Why not? Five people have been murdered and you don't even have one suspect? I don't understand it. I really don't."

Later that day, Sims was sitting in the study thinking that he did not understand it either.

Five professors murdered in less than two weeks and you don't have one suspect? Maybe it is a case of incompetence—not the Chairman's, but yours.

"Alright, none of that," Sims said aloud.

He was good at beating himself up, and once he started, he tended to go on and on to the point of complete depression. Now is when he thought about the little vials in his bedroom and the syringes that lay beside them. They could so easily take away the sharp edges of these blows. He could be moderate. He had often been moderate in the past.

He picked up the phone and dialed Abby's number.

"Hello, beautiful," he said.

"Hey there."

"Ready to go to Bonnie Bay?"

"Just say the word."

"The word."

She laughed.

42

At noon Goode was sitting in his den. He fretted a bit that they might find his fingerprints at Zeltner's, but not a lot. He knew he was not in any database. He clicked on the news. Every television station in Charleston was having hourly updates about his work. He was trying his best not to become conceited, but the fact was that he was winning. He had expected to win, but he had not envisioned the immensity of the force that had been put against him.

There must be hundreds, maybe thousands of cops trying to beat me. All working together, all constantly chattering to one another on cell phones, computers, radios. Many of these people must have very good minds, led by the best of all—Archibald Sims.

Suddenly Sims' picture flashed on the screen. Goode turned up the volume. The broadcaster looked excited. Had something changed?

" . . . and again the headline story just found out by our own Jessica Barns is that there is an apparent break in the College of Charleston murders. Jessica?"

"Yes, Charlie, I am here outside the English Department at the College of Charleston. I just spoke with Chairman Bates, who told me that a highly placed official in the investigation has stated that there appear to be, that is, appears to be, a major break in this ghastly series of murders . . . "

Goode got out of his chair and squatted in front of the television.

" . . . as you know, officials have been tightlipped from the very beginning . . . "

"Alright. What have they found out?"

" . . . even now, they are extremely cautious . . . "

"Yes, yes, yes. What has been found out?" he repeated, a little more loudly.

" . . . though when speaking to me, Chairman Bates seemed visibly more relaxed, he emphasized . . . "

"You blathering idiot. What is the break? Stop temporizing. What the hell is it?"

"Now neither Chester Bates nor any other source that I have spoke to . . ."

"'That you have *spoke* to'? Illiterate! You are completely illiterate!"

" . . . will confirm or deny, except to say that there has been a major break. Again, what that break is—no one will say."

"Because it's all a ruse!" Goode screamed. "There hasn't *been* a major break. This is all a desperate ruse to rattle me, to make me stop my work. Nothing has been discovered. Absolutely nothing."

He turned the television off.

It's Sims. He's playing with me. He set up this fake story to rattle me. Well, maybe I'll rattle him. Yeah, that's what I'll do. I'll just drop by his house for a little visit.

He went to the kitchen and put the kettle on. He patted the refrigerator. He looked at the two drums. He had already unscrewed the caps and the kitchen was reeking of formalin, but he knew he had to get used to it.

He made his cup of tea and sat looking at the work in front of him. It was going to be long and hard. He had actually thought of kidnapping some kid to do it, but then he would have had to kill him.

He finished his tea and picked up the piece of garden hose from the kitchen table. He would stick it into the drum, siphon the formalin into a five-gallon bucket and fill the aquarium.

The doorbell rang and he jumped. *Who can that be?*

Stung by the interruption, he looked at his watch and squatted down, putting his arms around himself. His mind raced. Had he made a call to a repairman? Was it the mailman? Was it the cops? Hugging his knees, he sat unable to move.

The doorbell rang again.

A major break in the investigation the news said. Have they found me?

Goode sat for a few seconds, then forced himself up. He grabbed a steak knife and went to the door. When he opened it, a UPS man was halfway back to his truck.

"Yes?" he yelled.

"Got a package for a Mister Taylor."

Goode studied the UPS man. *You're not a cop.*

"I'm Robert Taylor."

He presented the package with a grunt. He seemed exasperated.

"May I see some ID?"

Goode pulled one of the fake ones out of his wallet.

"If you could just sign this, please."

Goode felt his head shake a bit. He signed and took the package.

"Sorry, sir. Things are hectic."

He nodded and closed the door.

Politeness goes a long way.

He set the package down on the sofa and looked at the return address: Red Wood, Oregon.He cut off the brown paper and lifted the lid of a small wooden box.

Using the tip of the knife, he picked the paper open.

There were two of them, a brownish pink color, one of them larger than the other.

Ears. Human ears.

Goode put both hands to his mouth. He screamed with laughter. He had completely forgotten that he had sent them away—the ears of Finch and Owens. Once he realized he would not need them, he had found the name of a good taxidermist on the web. He remembered the ad: "We preserve anything." So he sent the ears and used a different name just in case.

He went back to the kitchen to finish filling the aquarium. Then he was going to Sims' house. He would not touch Sims, but he would touch his family. And how he would touch them.

43

Sims, Abby, and Cooper arrived on Edisto Island around four in the afternoon. It was terribly hot, 98 degrees and a hundred percent humidity.

Sims' Jeep passed the Old Post Office, crossed the bridge, and turned right onto Peter's Point Road. The great oak trees on either side provided some shade. The palmettos, oleanders, honeysuckle and blackberry bushes were so thick that they were more jungle than forest.

He stopped at the gate that led into the plantation.

There stood two massive brick columns with a ten-foot-tall wrought iron gate running between them.

He pressed a button on the dashboard and the gate began to slide open.

"Dad, can't we do something about the gate?" Cooper asked.

"What's the matter with it?" Sims asked.

"Oh, man, it's totally slow."

"Well, I don't think it's totally slow. Totally slow means it wouldn't move at all."

"It's pretty slow," Abby said.

"Why do we have to be in such a rush? Why can't we just take our time? Besides, it gives me a moment to observe."

"Observe what?" Cooper asked.

Sims pointed through the bars creeping by. To the left and right of the dirt road, they could just make out the tomato field.

"I didn't know you were going to plant them there, Dad."

"It's the best place for tomatoes. Lots of sun, deep topsoil, good drainage."

"Yeah, but where am I going to ride my dirt bike?"

"Gee, I don't know, Coop. You've only got another seven hundred acres."

"Not cleared off."

"Sounds like a good summer project for you."

"Yeah, right."

They passed through the gate, which automatically closed behind them.

Sims drove about fifty feet and then got out of the air-conditioned car. The heat and humidity descended upon him like a load of wet cotton.

He extended his arms. "Look at this. It's beautiful. It even smells different—the air."

Cooper lowered a window. "It smells different?"

"Get out of the car."

"Oh, Dad."

"Come on, come on, come on. Everybody out."

Abby and Cooper climbed out of the car into the wet heat of the island.

"Take a deep breath," Sims said. "Get a good lungful of it and tell me what you smell."

"Pluff mud," Cooper said.

"More," said Sims.

"All I smell is pluff mud."

"It does smell very green," Abby said.

Sims rushed her and swung her around in his arms.

"Brilliant. What a brilliant description. That's it precisely. The air smells green. It doesn't smell like pesticide and chemicals. It smells like living, green plants, and sunshine and rain. Isn't it splendid?"

Sims put Abby down and waded out into the field of plants. They were over a foot high now and stretched all the way to the edge of the jungle.

"I like him better when he's depressed," Cooper said.

"Coop."

"It's like he gets *so* into things."

"It means he's happy."

They stayed another few minutes while Sims explained all the chemicals that would be omitted from the field and then got back into the car. Sims insisted the air conditioner be turned off and the windows let down.

The car turned left and then made what the family called the Big Right: a dirt road lay between two rows of live oaks. There were forty of them. Their trunks were four or five feet around and their branches collected and interwove overhead creating a tunnel of shade. At the end of the tunnel sat the house called Bonnie Bay.

Square and Georgian with eight columns, the mansion had been built by Sims' great-great-grandfather in 1820. It was constructed of red brick and granite. The vast white frieze above the columns was decorated with a Greek meander. Sims guided the car into the semicircle of crushed oyster shells, which gleamed white and blue in the island sunlight.

He jumped out of the car and ran up the brick staircase and threw open the ancient door.

"Hello," he yelled.

"He's like a boy down here," Abby said.

"Tell me about it," Cooper muttered.

As Abby and Cooper pulled suitcases from the trunk of the car, they heard Sims calling them from the front door.

"Hey, y'all got to come see this. Hurry."

Cooper turned to Abby. "I don't know if I can deal with this all weekend."

"Oh, come on, now," Abby said.

They carried the bags up the staircase and into the great hall.

Pink was walking towards them, holding out the edge of her white apron. "It's late in the year. I'm surprised to see them."

The apron had a squirming belly in the center of it.

"What is it?" Cooper asked.

"You better have a look," Pink said.

"This is not some sort of like weird joke is it?"

"Come on, boy."

"Abby, why don't you go first?"

"You go right ahead, Coop."

He peered down into the apron.

44

"Baby ducks," Cooper said.

"They called ducklings," said Pink.

"Baby ducklings."

Pink shook her head, bent down, and opened her apron.

Seven brown and yellow ducklings swirled onto the floor, shivering and peeping.

"Now watch this," Sims said. He leaned over the ducks and blew a breath upon them. He started walking backwards.

The yellow puddle of ducklings, peeping louder than ever, began to follow him.

He moved faster, taking big steps, extending his arms, wriggling his fingers. "You are in my power. Follow."

"Hey, Dad, where did you learn to do that?"

"The Duck School of Hypnosis. I command you all to follow me."

The faster Sims retreated, the faster the ducklings pursued, until he stopped and they stormed his feet.

"I've never seen anything like it," Abby said.

"Imprinting," Sims said. "For the first few days after birth they will follow any movement."

Abby and Cooper picked up ducklings and brought them close to their faces to nuzzle.

Pink was watching with her arms folded over her bosom. She was wearing a long, print dress and her white apron. Around her neck was a string of blue shells.

"What's for supper?" Sims asked.

"I ain't the cook."

"I'm cooking, but you were supposed to be catching."

"You know what's in that creek well as I do."

"Shrimp?"

"Shrimp and more shrimp."

"You caught a lot?"

"Eleven pounds in seven throws."

Sims clapped his hands, cleared his voice. "Duck lovers of the world, listen up. Tonight I will make the shrimp feast."

"I don't think you've made it for me," Abby said. "What's in it?"

"The feast goes from the simple to the complex: shrimp soup, boiled shrimp, fried shrimp, and then the French master-pieces: *Buisson d'écrevisses cadinalisées* and *Gratin de queues d'écrevisses.*"

"Good heavens, I can't even pronounce them."

"By ten o'clock tonight the names of the dishes will roll off your tongue."

Cooper helped Pink gather the ducklings, while Sims and Abby went upstairs for a nap.

The old mansion had eight bedrooms. Each was named for one of the flowering plants found on Edisto Island. Abby always stayed in the Azalea Room, Sims in the Honeysuckle.

At half past five, Sims got up worrying about the air conditioning. He had put in a vast system fifteen years ago. Alice had objected, believing air conditioning would ruin the ambiance of Bonnie Bay. He had stated that the ambiance of the house was heat, humidity, and mildew.

He went checking the various thermostats. The temperature was around seventy-six, which was as cool as the place would get on a hot day.

Downstairs he went into the family room. Large windows looked out over the violet grass of the marsh that extended to the edge of Bohicket Creek, which ran all the way to the sea. He went to the bar and made himself a drink: Bombay Gin and tonic. He sat down in a chair and looked out the windows. In one corner of them was a host of no-see-ums. They were tiny, almost invisible, gnats that inflicted a stinging bite. The island was infested with them, though they usually only appeared near dusk.

Sims sipped his drink, thinking about Cupid. He prayed that he was right, that Cupid's slaughter was over.

Abby entered the room. She was wearing white shorts, a short-sleeve white silk blouse, and DayGlo flipflops. Her blond hair was knotted in a bob on the back of her head.

"Alright now," she said. "No thinking about the case."

"I promise."

"What are you drinking?"

"G and T."

"I'll have one too."

He went behind the stainless steel bar. It was completely out of place in the house. It was Norwegian. He had ordered it out of a magazine. It had taken him and two carpenters five days to get the bar set up, but it worked: bright and shiny with steel bar stools and countertops.

He handed her the drink. "You know what?"

"What?"

"We should go sit on the dock."

"What, you leave the air conditioning?"

"Well, there's a sea breeze."

"I'm all for it."

Sims led the way.

On the back porch, they ran into Cooper. He was shirtless, barefoot, wearing a pair of cutoff blue jeans.

"Hey, Dad, I ran into Billy Talbot. He wants me to spend the night at his house."

"That's fine, but you're going to be here for dinner, right?"

"Dude, I'm not about to miss the shrimp feast."

"Also, why don't you help Pink peel the shrimp?"

"Aw, come on, I was going to take the boat out."

"You can do that later. Hit the shrimp," Sims said.

Cooper saluted.

45

The smell of the formalin was really getting to Goode now. His eyes were watering, and his nose burned.

Time for a shower.

While scrubbing away the odor, he began thinking about Roger Neuman. He had gone to see him after Finch and Owens had gutted him. He remembered pleading: "I just don't understand. I met with them every month for almost a year. They didn't raise any objections."

Neuman was a tall and thin man with orange hair. He was working out on a stair climber on his back porch. He stank. "They didn't raise any objections because they probably had not been reading your submissions."

"They weren't reading my work?"

"No."

"Why? It was typed, double-spaced."

"Because professors are lazy. Most of us never read something until it is finished."

"So they never looked at it until the final draft?"

"Probably."

"Both of them told me they were giving you copies of what they were reading."

"The only thing I saw was the completed manuscript."

"What do you think of it?"

"I haven't read it."

Neuman stepped off the machine, grabbed a towel, then sank into a large hammock.

"You haven't read it either?"

"Sorry."

"Look, I brought a copy with me."

"Goode, there's just no point. Finch hates the work. Even if I read it and liked it, there's nothing I can do. Finch has the final say. I will have to vote against you."

"Please, it's my whole life . . . "

"You really must stop begging. It's unbecoming. Do you exercise?"

"What?"

"Do you exercise?"

"No."

"I exercise every day at the same time for at least forty minutes. Then I sleep, right here. Fresh air, exercise, very important to health. Go away now. Forget about working here. It's a nest of vipers."

Yes, it was a nest of vipers, and Goode was going to kill another one. He dried off and stepped into his bedroom. He unlocked a trunk and pulled out a narrow box. He opened it and ran his finger down the long weapon. He had used it twice in Vietnam. It was silent, fast, sleek, utterly reliable. One time right through the ear, right through the eardrum eight inches into the brain. There was little blood. The eardrum held it back. He could clean up Neuman with the corner of a handkerchief.

Thank goodness for dependability. Thank goodness for faithfulness.

He held it against his cheek and smiled.

46

As the last of light disappeared, Sims and Abby finished up a second drink on the dock. They sat side by side in weathered rocking chairs. He was holding her hand. In the first rush of alcohol they had talked rapidly, happily, like two teenagers, about everything and nothing. Now they simply rocked and listened to the marsh settling into night: the farewell cries of egrets and cranes and herons, the spray of a porpoise blowing in the backwater, the sound of shrimp disturbed and clattering on the surface of the tide, a cowbell ringing in some lonely glen.

"We should come here more often," Abby said.

He looked at her in the twilight. Her blond hair moved in the sea breeze, and her blue eyes gathered and held the very last of the invisible sun.

"Don't you think?" she asked, squeezing his hand.

He said nothing.

"Hamp?"

"Yes?"

"Are you listening to me?"

"Abby, there's something I must confess to you."

She pulled her hand from his. "What is it?"

"I've never made it."

"You've never made it?"

"What I boasted about earlier."

"I really don't know what you're talking about."

"*Buisson d'ecrevisses cardinalisees.*"

"Oh, you are awful. I thought you had some big secret."

"I have made the *gratin* though."

"Don't be playing with my head now."

"I'm sorry. I was just teasing." He took her hand and kissed her, then put his face against her soft cheek.

They kissed again and Sims felt the first sting on the back of his neck. Then he heard them singing, right under the dock.

"I think we're going to have to make a run for the house."

"So you can brush up on the *buisson*?"

"So we can not get eaten up by the no-see-ums."

"Ouch," Abby said and slapped her calf.

"Ready?"

"Ready."

He held her hand and dashed down the dock, following the row of lights on either side of the planks.

Inside the house, the big kitchen was bright and cheery. The floor was pine boards a foot wide. Sims had just replaced the old cabinets with new ones, French provincial. There were now Corian countertops and a work island with an old-style enamel sink in the middle. Pink was standing in front of a pile of gray shrimp.

"That boy didn't help me much," she said.

"Did he help at all?" Sims asked.

"He helped and he didn't help."

"In what way?"

"Well, he peeled about a pound, then throwed them in a pan and ate'm up."

"No seasoning?"

"Hamp, really. He's supposed to be helping Pink," Abby said.

"Well, he did have some seasoning, if you want to call it seasoning," Pink said.

Sims raised a finger and smiled as if he had discovered something. "Organic butter?"

"Ketchup."

"Ketchup?"

"That's what I said."

"My son has no taste." He sighed. "But no matter, we will now begin our sojourn into *gratin dequeves d'ecrevisses.*"

"Well, you sojourn ahead," Pink said. Her bare feet soughed across the pine.

"Pink, are you eating with us tonight?"

"Look here, Hamp, I'm eating boiled shrimp, not that fancy cheese shrimp, and I'm eating it at suppertime, not midnight."

"You can always change your mind," Sims said, but she had left the room.

"I really don't approve of Cooper's behavior," Abby said.

"I know. Ketchup is quite unforgivable."

"Hamp."

"Just kidding."

"He's spoiled. It is one of the reasons—one of the many—that we should not have servants."

He did not want to have a fight, so he began to assemble the ingredients.

"The most time-consuming element—*court bouillon*—has been made ahead," he said opening the refrigerator door.

"By whom?"

"By me."

"Are you sure?"

"Implying that I sent Pink down here a day early to pick, clean, boil, and strain the vegetables?"

"Yes," Abby said, raising her hands in the air, palms turned up and fingers spread.

"Well, she didn't do the work. I did. I always make a lot, then freeze it in smaller containers. Satisfied?"

"No."

He jammed his hands down into his pockets and dropped his head. "What do you want me to do, Abby? Issue an Emancipation Proclamation?"

"I really, really, really detest that tone in your voice."

She stormed out of the kitchen.

47

Sims slumped in a chair and looked at the big, empty fireplace. Sometimes he didn't think it was going to work at all. There was the age difference, obviously, but other things kept popping up: her secrecy about Jack, her temper, which would flare unexpectedly, and her attempts to change the way he lived his life. He knew he loved her, but sometimes he feared that he did not like her. This was something new for him. He had thought that if you loved someone, naturally you liked them. This was the way things had been between him and Alice. He loved her and he liked her. In fact, in the last years of their marriage, his liking turned into admiration. He had truly admired Alice. She was patient, practical, dependable, and kind.

The last of these attributes, he believed, was the most precious. Alice had always been kind to him. If he repeated himself too often, she did not chastise him. If he remembered something incorrectly or made some logical error in an explanation or simply woke up in a vinegary mood, she never took him to task, never raced to take advantage of his weaknesses. He wondered if Abby could become kind. There would be no future for them if she could not. He was certain of it.

Wearily, he got up from the chair and started the *gratin.* Cooking always helped. He could lose himself in it. It was not as good as Tai Chi, but right now it was what he needed.

Sims poured the *court bouillon* into a big pot. He threw in the shrimp and simmered them for five minutes. He drained the shrimp and removed the red tails. Quickly he made a basic *béchamel.* Using a mallet and a wooden board, he pulverized six tablespoons of shrimp shells. He mixed these with an equal amount of butter and forced the mixture through a sieve.

He melted more butter in a nonstick pan, sautéed the shrimp, added cognac, and touched it with a match. The sweet, bitter smell drove away his domestic despair. He sliced black truffle and mushrooms and threw them into the orange flame of cognac. He poured cream into the *béchamel* and heated the sauce slowly, spooning in the shrimp-shell butter with care.

He put the shrimp into three separate baking dishes and then covered them with the shell sauce. He lavished the mixture with grated Gruyère cheese, stuck the dishes in a preheated 400-degree oven, and browned the tops.

As he opened the oven door, Abby came back. "Smells good."

Her voice startled him.

"Did I scare you?"

"Didn't hear you coming."

"I'm sorry."

"It's okay. I lose myself a bit in cooking."

"I'm sorry for my little lecture."

"You're quite right about that tone of voice. I don't like it either."

Abby put her arms around him and he rocked her back and forth.

"I don't want to change you."

"Well, I could use some changes."

"Not very many."

He hugged her a while longer, then said, "I think we should sleep together tonight."

"Well, we'll have to do what we did before," Abby said.

"Refresh my memory."

"Big robes, bare feet, avoid squeaking boards."

"Ah, yes, I do remember."

While Sims put on a pot of Edisto Island Rice, Abby set the table. Twenty minutes later, they sat down. He ladled the *gratin* over the mound of fluffy rice in each plate. The sauce of shrimp and cheese was a faint orange color with dark bits of truffle and mushroom. They ate quickly, almost absurdly. He thought of a scene in *Tom Jones*. As soon as they were finished, he took her hand and they rushed upstairs, making sure to take off their shoes on the way.

At the door to his bedroom, Abby stopped him.

"What do we do if we get caught?"

"Deny everything."

"Everything?"

"Everything except . . . I love you, Abby."

"I love you too."

48

At 9:30 p.m., Goode stood in front of the house on East Bay Street. Sims' house. He was astonished at the immensity of it.

This guy's not a policeman. He's not a cop. Cops rent shoddy apartments or live in crummy cracker boxes, even trailers. Sims is some kind of imposter.

An hour earlier Goode had found Sims' phone number in the book. He was surprised that such a well-known detective would list his number and address publicly. He had called and a boy had answered. Goode said that he was Sergeant Smalls and that he needed to speak to the Inspector. The boy said that Abbagail and Mr. Sims were out of town and would not be back until the following day, but if it was important, he would give him Sims' cell number.

Goode was shocked at all the information that came to him so easily. What was it with Sims? Did he think he was immortal? Did he think that no one could get to him?

Well, then the great sleuth needs a little lesson in humility.

He walked around to the back of the house. The yard was surrounded by an eight-foot-high brick wall.

Finally a little caution.

He set down his briefcase, tugged on his gloves. He put his hands on his hips and cocked his head to the left, listening: cicadas and city traffic and the clicking of bats flying beneath a streetlight.

He opened the briefcase and found his penlight and studied his tools: glass cutter, suction cup, a small hand drill, gloves, and of course, his father's straight razor. He held it up in the moonlight and smiled at the dim, cool glow of the blade.

He looked at the wall. He wondered if broken glass had been set into the top row of cement. It was something that they did in Charleston. He remembered when he had first come to the city and how it had surprised him—great mansions surrounded by magnificent brick walls, but on the top of them broken bottles or shards of glass protruding from the bricks.

Using his penlight, Goode searched the top of the wall. It

was smooth. He put the razor back into the briefcase, closed it, and coiled his legs beneath him.

With one leap he made it. He threw a leg over and lay still. Just as he was about to move, the back porch light came on.

A teenager closed the door. He went down the back steps, tossing a set of keys in his right hand, and walked to the gate. He punched some numbers into the security pad, then backed the car out into the street.

Goode slipped down the wall and ran to the back porch. He twisted the handle. The door was not locked.

What idiots.

He walked through the kitchen and out into the hall. There were a couple of lights burning. He listened for some time. He wanted to be sure no one was in the house.

After a few minutes, he stepped down the hall, staying close to the left hand wall. The rooms of the house were enormous, the ceilings twenty feet high.

Once he had found out that the family was gone, he had changed his plan. He knew it was dangerous. He knew he was taking a number of chances, but he also believed in all his talents, in all his instincts. It was also exciting.

Who will it be? The boy or the woman? Or maybe someone else. Someone I don't know about. Like some doddering old aunt or uncle.

The one thing he did know was that his dreadful deed must take place where the person felt most secure—in the bedroom.

He checked the main floor and then silently mounted the staircase. At the top, he smelled the difference. This is where they slept and bathed and made love. Walking down the hall, he breathed in the fragrances of the family's intimacies. He smelled shoes and socks, mothballs and clothes, soaps and colognes and old quilts stacked in linen closets.

One room in particular attracted him with a rich aroma of perfume. He stepped inside. It was dark, but he smelled nail-polish remover and scented candles and the oily brightness of hairbrushes.

This must be Abbagail's room.

His penlight danced around in the darkness until he found a double bed, nightstands and lamps, and nearby a vanity glittering with bottles and brushes and combs.

He was troubled by only one thing. There were no closets in the room. There was no place to hide and wait. He knelt down by the bed, looked underneath it. He could fit there, but how predictable, awkward too. He would have to grab her arm or leg and then she would struggle and scream. Surely there was something else.

He stepped deeper into the room and his penlight discovered it: an armoire. It was small with two doors. He opened them and the smell of her enveloped him.

What beautiful clothes, he thought. He ran his hands over the silk and gabardine and linen dresses.

Oh what it must feel like to be Abbagail.

The idea occurred to him then. He began taking off his clothes. He stripped completely naked. He felt for the right one. It was silk. He pulled it off the hanger, stepped away from the armoire, and slipped into it. His flesh turned to goose bumps.

The dress was too long, but he didn't care. He danced about the room, danced in complete darkness, danced as if he were Abbagail.

I want more. I want more more more.

Goode sat down at the vanity. He lit one little candle. He knew no one could see it from outside. The candle smelled like vanilla. He looked into the mirror. First he put on lipstick, then mascara, and finally a little blush.

Why, I'm beautiful. I really am beautiful.

He turned his face from side to side and smiled and batted his eyelashes.

He sat at the vanity a while longer, then decided he needed to get into position. The boy might return at any time. He blew out the candle and went to the armoire. He put his briefcase inside, then closed the doors. He held his razor and snuggled down into a stack of luscious blouses.

49

Sims, Abby, and Cooper arrived back home around one o'clock in the afternoon. They rolled halfway down the driveway, but then had to stop. Sims' old Bentley sat in the middle of the drive.

"I was afraid of something like this," Abby said.

"Oh, I wouldn't worry about it," Sims said. "He probably just went for a little drive."

"I explicitly told him not to use the car unless there was an emergency."

"Maybe he had a Big Mac attack," Cooper said.

Abby took her keys out of her purse, got out of the car, and began striding toward the house.

"Take it easy on him," Sims called after her.

As Abby passed by the car, she glanced inside. Jack was laid out on the front seat.

She jerked open the car door. "Jack Young."

He did not move.

Abby reached and grabbed his ankle.

Still no response.

She climbed inside and shook his shoulder. Then she saw it—a well of blood in the hollow of his throat.

She screamed.

Sims ran to the car and threw open the door.

Jack's eyes were half open and stared towards the car roof.

Sims knelt down and felt his carotid artery for a pulse. Nothing.

Abby pressed her hands to her face and began screaming. "Is he alright? Is he alright? Jack? Jack?"

Still kneeling, Sims got his phone and called 911. He went around to the other side of the car and pulled Abby out. She was flailing her arms and screaming.

The EMS truck arrived in three minutes. Sims held Abby and pointed to the car. The paramedics pulled the body out and laid it on the grass.

"Cooper, get on into the house," Sims said.

"Dad, I can . . . "

"Get in the house."

The paramedics were working on Jack. One was giving mouth-to-mouth while the other pounded his chest.

"I think his throat's been cut," Sims yelled to them.

"Oh, no," Abby sobbed. "Oh, my dear God, no."

She collapsed into Sims' arms.

Cooper stood watching from the porch.

Sims saw his son. "Inside, right now."

"Dad, let me help."

"You can't. Now go upstairs to your room."

Cooper slipped his key into the lock and entered the front door.

50

Goode had drifted off, lulled by the silence of the house, when the sound of a siren began far off and came closer and closer and finally shattered the darkness he crouched in.

Inside the armoire, he listened to the commotion outside. Then he heard another sound—the popping of stairs. Someone was coming. He sat upright and prepared himself.

Who is it? Abby? Oh, I hope it's Abby. Please come into your room. Please open these doors.

He put his ear against the smooth wood of the armoire. For a moment he could hear nothing, then he heard steps. This time in the hall. He leaned into the door, holding the razor in his right hand. He was sweating and grinding his teeth.

Whoever it was passed the room and continued down the hall.

He heard a door close. *What to do now?* Someone had entered the house. He could lie there and wait for Abby, or he could go after whoever was upstairs. All his instincts told him to go after the person who was so close.

He opened the door, and it creaked.

Damn it!

He waited a few seconds, regained his composure, then slipped out of the armoire on all fours, rose to his feet, and in two silent strides stood at the door of the room. He listened, his ear to the door, and slowly opened it and looked up and down the hall. All the doors were open except one at the very end. He moved towards it, hoping not to make any sound that would give him away.

A big, red stop sign was nailed to the outside of the door. *So, this must be the kid's room—Cooper's.* He had read his name in the paper.

Suddenly, Goode became apprehensive. Was this a warning to him? Was something trying to tell him not to enter? To return to Abby's room?

He considered, then put his ear against the door. He could hear a shower running. *Cooper. It has to be Cooper.*

Perfect. Just like Psycho. *I slip in and get him in the shower. I always wanted to hit somebody like that. Complete vulnerability. Hitchcock was a genius.*

Goode opened the door and glanced around.

A boy's room, for sure.

Deer head on the wall. Gun case in the corner. Several posters of rock stars. A bench and rack of weights.

He looked at the door to the shower.

From below a voice called. "Cooper?"

Goode froze.

It was Sims' voice, louder this time.

"Cooper?"

The shower cut off.

"Hey, Cooper?"

Goode heard the curtain slide open.

The boy bounded out of the bathroom and into the hall.

Damn, another door, another room?

"Dad?"

"Ice! From the bar!"

Goode pressed himself beside the door. *Come back to your room, boy. You need a pair of britches.*

But he didn't. Goode heard him running down the hall, almost falling down the stairs.

Goode didn't understand it. Did he run out there naked? He went into the hall and stood beside the window and the long curtains that covered it. He opened them just in time to see Cooper running into the front yard with a bucket of ice. He was wearing a robe.

What kind of kid keeps a robe in his bathroom? I never did that. Prissy little creep.

Goode watched as the paramedics loaded someone into the ambulance, which immediately took off.

Sims and Cooper helped Abby to the Bentley. She was holding a white towel to her face.

They followed the ambulance.

He stood by the curtains a while. He wasn't going to get mad about it. He had only missed by a few seconds. Next time—and there would be a next time—he would get one of them.

51

At Roper Hospital, the Emergency Room doctors determined that Jack Young had OD'd on heroin. There was a large cut in the bottom of his chin that had come from some kind of blunt trauma—a fall or perhaps a fight. Sims and Abbagail stayed with him until he was stabilized.

Once Abby was certain her son was alright, though unconscious, she turned to Sims.

"I could use a drink," she said.

"I could use a double," said Sims.

"I could use a triple," the doctor said as he tied off the last stitch under Jack's chin.

They took Cooper to a friend's house, then went to the bar in Hyman's Seafood. The place smelled of oysters and lemon and the deep-fat fryer. They were drinking Ketel One martinis.

"I don't think I'll ever be able to trust him," Abby said.

"He's a kid. He screwed up. Every kid screws up," Sims said.

"Except Cooper."

"I could tell you a few stories."

"Do you know you have ants in your car?"

"Yes."

"A lot of ants."

"They have a nest in my car."

"Care to explain?"

"Long story."

They killed their drinks and ordered two more along with a bowl of boiled crabs.

"What do you think I should do with him?" Abby asked.

"Get him back in the program. Start over."

She leaned over and kissed him. "You're so good to put up with all of this."

When they had finished lunch, Sims dropped her off at her apartment, then went to police headquarters. Finally there was new evidence. The SBI in North Carolina had called to say that they had found several hairs beneath Zeltner's fingernails. It didn't mean very much. Mitochondrial DNA analysis could take sixty days or even more. Sims needed a break now.

He kept an afternoon meeting with the detectives: no solid leads, no suspects. The men left looking dispirited. Tuttle was sitting across the desk in a Hart Schaffner and Marx suit, which was drastically too big.

"Where did you get that?" Sims asked.

"Ole Doc Townsend had a yard sale this morning."

"It is ridiculously ill-fitting."

"Well, it's a little loose."

"Townsend weighs three hundred fifty pounds, Tom."

"So, I'll get it taken up."

"It doesn't need to be taken up, it needs to be cut in half."

Lieutenant Harry Sacks came into the office. He was short and thin. "Hamp, I was going back over my interviews last night. I talked to this one fella . . . "

"When did you talk to him?"

"Two days ago. I interviewed four people that day, so it didn't hit me until I went over the report again. He said there was a guy who hated Finch."

"A lot of Finch's colleagues hated him."

"Yeah, that's it. This guy wasn't a professor. He was a student. A graduate student."

"So why did *he* hate Finch?"

"Apparently, Finch was head of his—hold on . . . ." Sacks glanced down at his report. "His dissertation committee. Yeah, I got 'he rejected his dissertation.' I don't exactly know what that means, but . . . "

"Could mean a lot. Did he threaten Finch?"

"No. He cried."

"He cried?"

"That's what he said, this Larry Wilcox. He said the guy broke down and cried like a baby."

"Did Wilcox know his name?"

"His first name, yeah. It was Jasper."

An hour later, Sims was sitting in Larry Wilcox's apartment at 121 Sheppard Street. It was a typical student place: beer cans on the floor, stacks of pizza boxes smelling of mold, pictures of nude girls tacked to the walls.

Wilcox was muscular and tan in a tank top and black running shorts.

Sims had been talking to him for only a few minutes.

"So, you had three conversations with this Jasper?"

"Three or four."

"Right after class?"

"Yeah."

"You didn't go out for a beer with him or anything?"

"The dude was really uptight, you know."

"Did he have any friends?"

"Not that I met."

"Oh, what class was it?"

"Pardon?"

"What class did you two share?"

"The Romantics."

"Which would consist of whom, Byron, Keats . . . ?"

"Hey, that's pretty good—and Shelley . . . "

"Yes, Shelley. Fine poet," Sims said.

"Oh, no, Mary Wollstonecraft. His wife. She's phat right now. In fact, Jasper was writing his dissertation about her."

Suddenly Sims saw a connection. "Could I trouble you for some water?"

Wilcox ran a hand over his shaven head. He opened a small refrigerator sitting by the sofa. "Sorry, I don't have any."

Sims glanced at the sink in the kitchen. "Just the regular . . . "

"Oh, tap water. You drink that stuff?"

"I think it's okay."

"Hey man, it'll eat the paint off a car."

"I'm not washing my car. I just want a little to drink. A very small glass."

Wilcox shrugged and went into the kitchen.

Sims was stunned by the possibility. The various crime scenes flew through his mind.

"I don't know if I have a glass."

"Anything will do—anything clean."

"Oh, yeah, before I forget about it, I mean, I'm not a detective or anything, but—all those professors that been killed? A couple were on his committee."

"You mean the Salary Committee?"

"I don't know about that. I'm talking about his dissertation committee. The one that trashed him."

Sims got up and went to the door of the kitchen. "How do you know who was on his dissertation committee?"

Wilcox was still looking. "He showed me the list. That was the day he got all upset and cried."

"Do you remember the names?"

"Well, like I said, some of them were the professors who've been killed. Finch, Whister, somebody else. Every dissertation committee is different, since the student usually picks the members. The department has all kinds of committees, so I'm sure it's just a coincidence, but I thought . . . ."

When Wilcox returned with the water, Sims had vanished.

52

Goode was sitting in ten pounds of rotting shrimp in his bathtub.

To be one you got to smell like one.

He had been in the shrimp for almost half an hour. He took two more handfuls and rubbed them again over his chest and arms.

I will not put them in my hair. If this isn't enough to make me smell like a shrimper, too bad.

He got up and into a pair of dirty khaki pants. He swirled an old tee shirt in the tub and pulled it on. He threw the shrimp into his ice cooler, on which he had already written in black magic marker: Shrimp For Sale.

He hid his ice pick and handsaw beneath the shrimp. He put on a stained, long-billed hat, grabbed the cooler, and got on his way.

He hoped Neuman had not changed his training hour.

Goode parked his car on Bogard Street. He wanted to be close to Neuman's house, but not too close. For a few seconds, he sat in the car. He had the windows down. He watched and listened. The sun was hammering everything with silent blows. He was sure the temperature was near a hundred. The smell of the shrimp drove him to move. He got the cooler out of the backseat. Holding it with both hands, he walked down Bogard and took a left onto Rutledge Avenue.

Even in the dreadful heat, even in the hot core of the afternoon, the tourists were still out. The wind was behind him. He watched a couple walking towards him. Their expressions changed. The woman actually put a handkerchief to her nose as he passed by. It made him laugh. He wanted to call something out. He shouldn't. He should just get on to Neuman's, but he couldn't help it.

"Shrimp for sale!" Goode yelled. "Fresh shrimp for sale!"

Three Indians heard him. They crossed the street and approached. The woman was wearing a sari, and the men were in white suits. Their faces curdled as they neared him.

"This is fresh shrimp?" one of them asked.

"Very fresh," Goode said.

"This does not smell very fresh."

"Well, you're probably just smelling me."

"Sorry?"

"You're probably smelling me. Been on the boat for two days. Haven't had a bath."

"Thank you very much. Thank you."

The trio walked away quickly.

Goode looked around, then darted into the driveway beside the house.

He set his cooler behind two gardenia bushes beside the garage. He stood and listened: the growl of skateboards, a bugle—someone practicing taps in a garden.

How appropriate. How truly appropriate.

Then he heard something close, a cadenced pounding.

The brick wall around the house was six feet high. He looked for an opening in the wall: a drainage pipe, electrical or gas lines.

There was nothing until he spotted several loose bricks. He made a hole and slithered through.

The back porch of the house was up a set of marble stairs, twelve to fourteen feet off the ground. It was covered by screen wire and trellised vines of morning glories.

Goode could see him jogging on his treadmill. He slipped to the steps and hid beneath them.

So cool here. So cool and dark.

He looked at his watch. He was a little late, but it was okay. He laid his saw on the ground. He could hear Neuman huffing and puffing above him. He pulled the ice pick from his belt and squatted down and stuck the tip of it into his ear.

This is the way it will be for you, professor. Very soon now. This is the way it will be for you.

53

Sims was waiting outside Chester Bates' office. He had made several phone calls, trying to find him. The chairman was supposed to be keeping office hours, but he wasn't. Sims was beginning to worry.

Finally, Bates came up the stairs and entered the room.

"Professor, I need some information. It's urgent. Do you remember a graduate student with a first name of Jasper?"

Bates held up his hands. "One second, Inspector. I'm just back from a swim and—for once—relaxed."

Bates got out his keys, sighed, mumbled, and opened his door.

Sims followed him. "I need to know his last name."

Bates sat down behind his desk. "You're investigating graduate students now?"

"Yes."

"Well, I hardly think . . . "

"His first name is Jasper."

"And he was a grad student in this department?"

"Correct."

"When?"

"A year or so ago."

"Inspector, at any given time we have fifty to sixty graduate students working on their PhDs. I doubt if I know even ten percent of their names. I need more information."

"His committee rejected his dissertation."

"They rejected it?"

"Yes."

"Are you sure? That very, very rarely happens . . . "

"I am certain it was rejected. Professor, this man is the prime suspect. We must move quickly."

Bates' eyes got large. He swiveled in his chair and began working the keyboard of his computer.

"We keep a list of PhD candidates filed under the name of their director."

Sims leaned over the desk.

The computer screen went black.

"Damn," Bates said.

"Can we use your secretary's?"

"No, the system is down. They sent us a message yesterday. Some kind of maintenance. We can access the file manually, but it will take some time. It's in the records building."

The two men walked quickly to a small building made of red brick. An ancient magnolia tree stood in front of the door.

Sims followed Bates through a maze of boxes and file cabinets that towered to the ceiling. They stopped before an elevator. Bates pushed *up*.

"Is there no other way to do this?" Sims asked.

"None that I know of."

"I also need the names of the professors who served on Jasper's committee."

"They should be in the same place."

The narrow elevator door slowly creaked open.

Sims felt like he was moving through water, like everything was slow and heavy.

They walked single-file to a room at the end of a corridor. Above the door was a sign: ENGLISH LANGUAGE AND LITERATURE.

Bates took out his keys and unlocked the door.

Ahead was another hallway, more bookshelves, and file cabinets.

"How much farther?" Sims asked.

"Down the hall. Up a flight of stairs."

54

Goode heard Neuman get off the treadmill. The boards of the porch creaked as he walked around, then there was a thud as he threw himself into the hammock. Goode listened to him swinging back and forth, the whine and pop of the ropes. He waited exactly ten minutes, then looked out into the empty yard. He went up the steps, thankful that they were marble and could not give him away. The porch, perhaps the screen door, would be another problem. He slipped into his gloves.

At the top of the steps, he stopped and looked through the screen and the morning glories into the shade of the porch.

Neuman was barely swinging now. He was lying on his side.

Gooded stood and waited another couple of minutes, until the hammock was still and he heard a soft snore.

Maybe I'll be really lucky. Maybe he doesn't like locks.

He pulled the door handle.

Nope.

Goode could see the latch at the top of the door. He took the ice pick, slid it along the edge, and gently pushed up. Open.

Closing his eyes, holding his breath, he pulled the door and it came to him without a sound.

He was on the porch. He felt incredibly nervous, but incredibly excited. He didn't want to blow this. He didn't want Neuman to wake. It would take away the fun. Sure, he could get him, but he wanted to get him while he slept. What would it be like for him? What would he be dreaming about—some blue-eyed sophomore, the two of them lying on a beach? Then comes a spectacular stroke of light? A scalding pain? Would it be something like that?

Goode tucked the ice pick into his belt. He extended his hands and put his weight on his heels. He wanted to expose as little of his feet as possible to the floor. He must reach Neuman in utter silence.

Balancing, he stepped forward on his heels and made it to the edge of the hammock. He was ecstatic. He wanted to do something, to play with him, but he did not allow himself this luxury. He took the ice pick from his belt and held it like a pen: thumb, index and middle fingers. He bent over the professor and looked into his ear. He could hear him snoring, feel the heat of exercise still coming off him.

He poised the ice pick one inch above the ear canal and punched.

Neuman shuddered and an arm shot out toward the wall.

Goode released his weapon. He crossed his arms and stared at the body. There was a tic here, a twitch there, and then he was still.

Goode waited a few more seconds. Then, using the palm of his hand, popped the ice pick as deep as he could, all the way to the handle.

Again, he waited, then pulled the ice pick out. A pulse of blood shot up, surprising him. He didn't remember this happening in Vietnam.

Doesn't matter. Things are going to be pretty messy with this guy anyway.

He unfastened his belt and got his hacksaw. He grabbed Neuman and turned him on his back. He adjusted the right leg to a convenient angle.

Goode arrived home and got his newest sewing done. It was time to become invisible now. He had gotten the idea from John Griffin's novel. He opened the medicine chest, pushed aside his morphine, and grabbed two containers. He emptied the white crystals of silver nitrate into the tub and poured in the alcohol. He got in the bath and smeared it all over himself. He shaved his buzz cut and scrubbed the top of his head with the liquid. When he got out, he did not dry off, but rather sat in front of the ultraviolet lamp.

55

On the third floor of the Records Building, Chester Bates pulled out a box marked CANDIDATES 1996—2002. He handed Sims several files.

"What am I looking for?" Sims asked.

"A file labeled DISSERTATION COMMITTEES."

The lights went out.

"I can't believe this," Bates said.

"Any emergency lighting? This have to do with system maintenance?"

"I don't know."

"Let's just sit a while," Sims said. He punched a button on his watch and the face lit up. "Let's give it a few minutes."

"Then what?"

"We take the box outside."

"We can't find our way out of here in the dark."

"We have to."

They waited for almost fifteen minutes, then the lights came back on, flickered, steadied.

The men worked the files.

Sims found six class rolls for 1999. He was reading when his cell went off.

"Cupid's started again," Tuttle said.

"What?"

"Professor Neuman. His maid just called. She's hysterical. She thinks he's still in the house."

"What do you mean?"

"Cupid's still in the house."

Though Rutledge Avenue was only a few blocks away, Sims drove. He arrived at the house just as Tuttle was running towards the front steps. At the bottom of them, the maid was sitting with her face in her hands.

Sims knelt in front of her, took her hand. There was blood on it. Her name was sewn on the front pocket of her white uniform.

"Mary, what happened?"

"He dead, he dead, he dead."

"I know this is hard, but you must try to calm down. Is the killer still in the house?"

"He dead. He cut up. Look." Her hands were smeared with blood to her elbows.

"Mary."

"I think he is. I think that man is."

"Where is Professor Neuman?"

"The back porch, all to pieces on the floor."

A squad car pulled up. Two officers ran up to Sims and Tuttle.

"You look after her," Sims said to the older of the men. "And you come with me."

Sims pulled his Glock from his pocket. He opened the front door with the young officer behind him.

He could see straight to the back doors leading to the porch.

"Want me to take the upstairs?" the officer asked.

"No. You take the rooms on the left. I'll take the right."

There were three rooms on each side of the hall. Sims stepped quickly into each of the right-hand rooms, then went to the double doors. He looked over his shoulder, but didn't see the kid.

"Hey," Sims said quietly.

Silence.

Why hadn't he asked the kid's name?

"Officer?"

Silence.

Sims moved back down towards the front door. He heard a voice, very soft. He couldn't make out the words.

"Officer," he said again.

"Inspector? Inspector Sims?"

Was that the kid? Or was it Cupid?

Sims extended the pistol in front of him.

He moved towards the voice.

56

In the middle room, Sims found the officer. He was staring at a wall.

A form lay there, an outline drawn in blood. It was a man, hastily done, but a ten-foot-tall man. Beneath his square feet, Cupid had scrawled: COMING SOON.

"What is your name?" Sims asked.

"Jones. Is that blood?"

"Yes."

Jones pushed up his hat with a thumb. He was white as sugar. "I don't deal so good with blood," Jones said.

"What?"

"It kinda makes me . . . "

Sims grabbed him before he went down. He set him in a chair.

Tuttle entered the room. "Cupid's not here. What happened to Jones?"

"Somewhat squeamish," Sims said, pointing at the wall.

"Oooooo."

"So, you don't think he's here?"

"Footprints down the back steps all in blood."

"Let's take a quick look upstairs anyway," Sims said.

The detectives checked the upstairs rooms and came down to the back porch.

Neuman was lying in the hammock. His legs had been cut off. The porch was blood.

Sims' phone buzzed.

"Jasper Goode," Bates said.

"Got an address?"

"P.O. Box 153, Highway 162."

"Get me everything else you can find."

Sims looked at Tuttle. "We have an address."

"Where?"

"Hollywood."

In Tuttle's car, Sims radioed headquarters to send a response team to Rutledge Avenue.

They arrived at the little blue house off Highway 162

in less than half an hour. A truck was in the driveway. Sims parked behind a clump of shrubs so the car couldn't be seen from the house.

"Maybe we should wait for backup," Tuttle said.

"Let's take him now."

They got out of the car, dashed across the lawn and onto the porch. Sims kicked open the door, yelling, "Police!"

Someone stepped out of a room.

Sims leveled his pistol between the eyes.

57

"Get out of my house! Get out of my home!"

"Inspector Sims, Charleston Police. Now, get your hands up."

"I certainly will not."

Tuttle came up from behind. "Hey, buddy."

Sims stepped closer. It was an old man: white hair, wrinkles, a cane.

Careful now. May be a disguise.

"Put your hands in the air," Sims said.

Tuttle grabbed him in a bear hug and cuffed him.

"Let go of me!" the old man yelled. "You let go of me!"

"What is your name?" Sims asked, getting close enough to smell him.

"John Thompson. What's *yours*?"

"I've already told you. *Sims.* Where's your wallet?"

"None of your damn business. Home invasion! Home invasion! Home invasion!"

Sims saw a wallet and car keys lying on a hall table. He found the driver's license: John Henry Thompson. Date of birth, 1926.

Sims went through the small house, but he already knew: wrong address. He came back into the living room, where the old man was sitting in a chair.

"Do you know a man named Jasper Goode?" Sims asked.

"Get out of my house! I'm calling the police!"

"We *are* the police," Tuttle said.

"Police! Police! Police!" Thompson yelled.

Sims took out his handcuff key.

Thompson was screeching. "Police! Police!"

"Now, Mister Thompson, if you will calm down . . . ."

Just then a squad car, siren blasting, pulled into the yard.

"See, there're the police. I knew they'd come. I got powers. I got all kinds of powers," the old man said.

Sims and Tuttle were sitting with John Thompson at

his kitchen table. He was calm and rational. Sims wanted to question him. They were drinking coffee and eating sweet potato pie.

" . . . so I'll say it one more time—y'all should have knocked. You didn't have to bust up my door. And who's going to pay for that? What if I had a gun?" Thompson asked.

"Mr. Thompson, we had to act fast, take the guy by surprise," Sims said. "There have been several *murders*."

"You already said that."

"Could I have another piece of that pie?" Tuttle asked.

"Sure," Thompson said. He cut him a slice.

"It's a shame a man can't eat for a living," Tuttle said.

"So you didn't know Jasper Goode at all?" Sims asked.

"No, I didn't know him. I met him a couple times."

"What did he look like?"

"Little bitty feller. Five feet tall. Can't be much over five feet. Might of weighed ninety pounds soaking wet. Go see for yourself."

"Pardon?" Sims asked.

"He lives two miles down the road."

"Goode does?"

"Do you need a hearing aid?"

"Do you know the address?"

"No, but you can't miss his house. Two miles down and painted red. The only red house out here."

58

At that moment, Goode was driving past Thompson's. He glanced at the police car, but didn't slow down. He knew what was going on. He had heard the siren. The cops found his old place. They were close now, but not close enough.

He felt giddy, nervous, almost nauseous with anticipation. He had gotten them all: Finch, Owens, Whister, Howard-Smith, Zeltner, and Neuman. There was only one more. He had not been on the dining room wall. He had appeared organically. There was something beautiful to it, something subtle and graceful. It was *art* really. You begin something, you make your plans, and then a lovely surprise occurs—like deconstruction. He wondered if it had been this way with Michelangelo. Would he be carving something, following his plans, and then suddenly find that he must cut a swirl here, chisel a striation there, or create some unforeseen finial?

He shrieked with laughter.

Somehow I have become an artist. I have become a sculptor.

Goode got through the worst of the five o'clock traffic and parked his car on South Battery. He grabbed his briefcase, which held duct tape, the saw, morphine, and half a bag of ice. He had started walking up East Bay when he saw a mobile news van pulled off to the side of the street. A reporter waited.

"Hey, what's going on?" Goode asked.

The reporter was tall and fat and wore a cowboy hat. He was sucking a purple popsicle. "Guess you haven't heard."

"Heard what?"

"The butcher killed another one."

"Another professor?"

"Yeah. Cut off his legs. Really gross."

"In this house?"

"No, this is Sims' place. Pretty nice for a cop, huh?"

A blond boy opened the front door and walked down to the bottom of the steps and halfway into the yard.

The reporter yelled: "Coop, hey, Cooper, look this way."

Goode went to the fence. He put an arm through and waved Cooper Sims towards him.

Hesitantly, the boy approached the miniscule black man.

Goode was feasting: long brown legs, khaki shorts, no shirt, with ripples in his belly and broad shoulders.

"Would you sign an autograph for me?" Goode asked.

"Will you go if I do?"

"Sure."

"Alright."

Cooper waited.

Goode smiled and did not move.

"Well, have you got a Sharpie?" Cooper asked.

"Oh, no, I'm sorry. I thought you would."

"Look, Mister, we need some space here, know what I'm saying?"

"Yes, yes, I do. I'm terribly sorry," Goode said. He waved goodbye and continued on.

59

Tuttle ran to the back of the house.

Sims opened the front door and yelled, "Jasper Goode! Police Department!"

There was this terrible stench.

Sims went into the den, where he found Tuttle standing silently.

In a tall case of bloody liquid, lit by two spot lamps, stood a man, or something like a man. The body was nude. Nothing was proportional, nothing worked together, except the legs. They matched and, like the arms, they had been expertly stitched to the massive and heavy torso whose nipples gleamed with rings. One arm was small and thin, the other hairy and big and blue. The arms and legs had been taped to the back wall of the aquarium. The corpse was headless, but something golden sat on the stump of neck.

Sims stepped closer.

A golden yarmulke had been sewn onto the neck like some sort of temporary cap.

He remembered the smell then—formalin, a chemical used to preserve dead tissue. It was bubbling and gurgling in the aquarium.

"His thesis was about Mary Wollstonecraft," Sims said. "He made his own creature, murder by murder, piece by piece, stitch by stitch."

He put his hand on the glass and stared up at it. He began to identify the different body parts and from whom they had come.

"Why isn't there a head?" Tuttle asked.

Sims broke away from his reverie. "I think you know."

"He's going to kill somebody else, isn't he?"

Sims went into the dining room. There were six portraits. He returned to look at the creature.

"We got to get on the horn, man. We got to put guards around the entire faculty."

"Just one member of the faculty," Sims said.

"Who?"

"Who would make a perfect head for this body?"

"I have no idea."

"The head of the department. The man who approved the decision of the Dissertation Committee. Chester Bates."

Sims gazed up at the corpse a while longer, then pulled out his cell.

Bates answered at his home.

"You must leave your house immediately, Professor."

"Why? What's happened?"

"Goode is coming for you."

"Where do I go?"

"Police Headquarters. Is there anyone else with you?"

"No."

"Then leave now. Do you understand?"

Sims called headquarters and told them to be ready to receive Bates. He explained nothing to them. He didn't want them involved.

He and Tuttle ran for the car.

60

Goode went around to the side of Bates' house. He had seen the old coal chute in the basement wall. He hoped it still worked. He had bought a can of WD-40. He set his briefcase down and looked around one more time. He knelt down before the small door in the foundation.

Running his hands across the iron, Goode felt the rust. He reached for the hinges. They were rusted too. He pulled the handle and the door partly opened. He sprayed the hinges with the WD-40, waited a few seconds, and pulled. The door creaked open. He crawled into the chute headfirst. He felt spider webs, felt the soot crumbling upon him, felt his heart beating.

The angle of the coal chute was steep, and he slid into the basement easily. He lay there for a couple of minutes, listening: music playing upstairs, a refrigerator humming in the basement, water running through a pipe.

He slowly stood, brushing filth from his face. He pulled the razor from his pocket.

Using his penlight, he found the staircase and made his way to the first floor.

Methodically he searched the house, room by room, closet by closet, nook by nook. At the end he collapsed into a chair.

No Bates. How could that be? This was his time to be at home.

At first he felt like crying. It would ruin everything. His sculpture would be unfinished. He felt the tears begin to come, but then suddenly an idea, a new inspiration. There was an even better finial. Much better.

And it was very near.

Goode leapt out of the chair, but before he left, he thought of something. He went into the kitchen, found a magic marker.

61

Sims and Tuttle searched Bates' house quickly. They went back to the entrance and looked out the windows towards the street.

"He'll wait for dark," Sims said. "He knows we've got everyone looking for him. He'll wait for night and creep inside."

"And we'll be waiting."

Sims saw it then—something scrawled beside a door. He stared a moment and then walked down. Written in black ink was a message: *If you can keep your head when all about you are losing theirs, then you'll be a man my son.*

For a few seconds he could not breathe, then he said softly, "He wants Cooper, Tom."

"What?"

"He wants Cooper."

They ran the three blocks to Sims' house. Halfway there, Tuttle fell, hurt his leg. "Go on!" he yelled. "Go on!"

62

Gun drawn, Sims sprinted the front steps and crashed through the door. He screamed out Cooper's name and then felt a massive shock to the back of his head. He went down to his knees and turned to see a small black man. Black as India ink.

"Well, I see you remember your Kipling," Goode said. He kicked the Glock from his hand, then knelt beside him.

Sims was losing consciousness.

"Don't worry. I'm not going to kill you. I made that decision some time ago. I just want you to rest for a while, Inspector. Night-night."

He rammed a hypodermic of morphine into Sims' jugular. He held him until he passed out.

Goode went back to the kitchen.

Abby was taped to a chair. There was a piece of duct tape across her mouth. She was alert.

"Hello, my dear. Your erudite boyfriend finally arrived."

Goode turned his attention to Cooper, who was taped down to the kitchen table. His eyes were closed. He had doped him. He patted the boy on the face. "Like father, like son. Everyone's quiet and resting now."

He picked up his hacksaw and gently turned the boy's head to the left.

There was a sound of shattering glass, and suddenly Goode's body rocked. A hole of blood bloomed between his eyes. He blinked. Crumpled.

Tuttle hobbled into the kitchen from the porch.

"Abby?"

Gently, he peeled the tape from her mouth.

She sobbed.

63

Epilogue

Sims spent two days in the hospital. Abby and Cooper were out in one.

The third day Sims woke up in his own room. The back of his head had been shaved and bandaged. It still throbbed.

The door opened and Tuttle came in.

"Archibald, you're looking better."

"I don't feel better. Where's Coop?"

"In the kitchen with Abby."

"Where did you get the gun?"

"Back porch."

"The thing hasn't been fired in a year."

"Did the trick."

"So, Goode dyed himself black?"

"Silver nitrate."

"I didn't know it could turn skin so dark."

"He enhanced it with something else. Maybe some kind of light. We're running tests."

Tuttle patted his hand. "Well, I'll let you rest. Need anything?"

"I'm fine."

As soon as Tuttle left, he drifted back to sleep.

Sometime later, there was a tap at the door.

"Hey, Dad, you awake?"

Cooper's voice, the youth and sweetness of it, made him smile.

The boy entered his room carrying a tray. He had a bandage on his neck.

"I made you breakfast."

Sims propped himself up in bed.

Cooper set the tray on the night table and laid three newspapers on his father's chest. "Did that guy—like, did he really make a monster?"

"Yes."

"Was it gross?"

"In every way."

"Is it still in his house?"

"I'm sure."

"Hey, Dad, could you like take me to see it?"

"No."

"Why?"

"Because it's—horrific."

"I know. I sort of get into things like that."

"What's for breakfast?" Sims asked.

"Your favorite: grits, quail eggs and venison sausage."

"I didn't know you could make grits?"

Cooper rubbed his eye. His hair was uncombed and Sims could tell he wasn't quite himself. "Well, Henry cooked the grits. He put his secret ingredient in it."

"Did you see what it was?" Sims asked.

"Nope."

"Henry has cooked grits for this family fifty years, and I still don't know how he gets the taste."

"How about a picture?"

"Maybe when I'm out of bed."

"Not you, the monster."

"No picture."

"Aw, Dad."

Sims reached for the tray, but Cooper got it and set it on the pile of newspapers. "There you go, Hero."

Sims shook his head.

On the way out, Cooper said: "Oh, the foreman called from Bonnie Bay. The tomato plants are dying. Some kind of bugs."

Sims sighed and then looked at his food. He ate the whole plate. Cooper was turning into a good cook.

Suddenly he remembered the first time he saw his son in the hospital. He was pink and wrinkled and so long. He remembered thinking, *Why, he's going to be taller than I am.*

Sims got out of bed. He was dizzy and wobbled his way to his grandfather's mirror. He looked at the wound on the back of his head. He looked at his eyes.

Somehow they were not the same.

Ben Greer, a native of South Carolina, published his first book of fiction at the age of twenty-six. *Slammer*, a novel based upon his experiences in a maximum security prison, received rave reviews.

Since the publication of this first novel, Greer has written and published three others: *Halloween, Time Loves a Hero,* and *The Loss of Heaven.* All his novels were extensively reviewed in the United States and Canada. Currently Ben Greer teaches at the University of South Carolina and is at work on his second Archibald Sims novel.